I0745641

his cosplayer

A LOVE GAMES NOVEL
by
ALLYSON LINDT

This book is a work of fiction.

While reference might be made to actual historical events or existing locations, the names, characters, places and incidents are either the product of the author's imagination or are used fictitiously, and any resemblance to actual persons, living or dead, business establishments, events, or locales is entirely coincidental.

Copyright © 2019 by Allyson Lindt
All Rights Reserved
ISBN: 9781949986655

No part of this publication may be reproduced, stored in a retrieval system, or transmitted in any form or by any means, electronic, mechanical, recording or otherwise, without the prior written permission of the author.

Manufactured in the United States of America
Acelette Press

For my eternal dragon

chapter one

Archer knocked back another swallow of beer and leaned forward on the butcher-block countertop, forearms resting on the wood. *Engagement party.* This hadn't been his most brilliant idea. Who threw an engagement party for their best friend and ex-girlfriend? *Me, obviously.* He took another drink.

Once upon a time, he would have fixed his gaze fixed on the woman standing across the room. She was tall, with long blonde hair, and surrounded by friends. Even in something as simple as a pair of jeans, Riley drew attention.

She was happier now than she'd ever been with him. He tried for weeks to figure out why it bugged him—they weren't meant to be. Tonight, the light haze of alcohol offered him a unique clarity.

If it had taken her a decade to figure out who she belonged with, then he'd wasted the on-again-off-again that had been their unstable relationship, thinking it should be him. His odds of finding someone he could make as happy as she was now had to be almost nonexistent.

Zane—Riley's fiancé and Archer's best friend since childhood—broke away from the group and crossed the hardwood which covered the open living room and kitchen. He stopped on the other side of the island and glanced over his shoulder at Riley, before giving Archer a half smile. "Thanks for the party. I know it hurts."

Archer set his bottle aside. He wasn't in the mood for a philosophical discussion about soul mates or finding *the one*, or how many times Riley had dumped him before he figured out she wasn't his one and only. He didn't care that a conversation like that wasn't manly; he was trying not to dwell. "I mean it when I say I'm okay with this."

"Hey, boys." Tori stepped up next to Archer. He'd met Tori through his sister. She and Jen had been in the same sorority years ago, and when Jen introduced her to Archer, they hit it off quickly. He'd owned his comic store long enough to know there were as many female fans as male, but regardless of gender, not a lot of them talked about books the way Tori did.

It didn't hurt she had curves that wouldn't quit, and she rocked a free T-shirt like no one's business.

She looked at Zane. "The group over there wants to know if you really hacked old Soviet missiles and disabled the warheads remotely." Her tone was cool.

"You're sure they don't want to hear a new story?" Zane turned back to Archer. "Thanks again." He made his way back to the small crowd on the other side of the room.

Not interested in another drink, Archer resumed his vigil, holding up the counter. He shouldn't stare—it wasn't like he cared—but he couldn't keep his gaze from drifting back to the happy couple. Zane dropped onto the couch against the far wall and tugged Riley into his lap. She didn't resist, falling with a squeal.

If Archer figured out why he and Riley never found that spark, he could do things better when he met the right woman.

Her fingers traced the white suede choker around her neck. The choker—which he hadn't seen her without since she'd gotten it—was new. The silver locket hanging from it was old; she'd had it since Zane gave it to her in high school.

That should've been another indicator she was meant to be with Zane.

"…and I think I'm going to see if bleach really does take the color out of Renaissance velvet." Tori's voice penetrated his wandering thoughts, and he whirled to face her.

"Wait. What?"

"Just wondering if you were listening."

He shook his head, to push away the past, and focused on Tori. "I'm sorry. What were you saying?"

"Don't worry about it. I asked if you were going to spend the entire night staring." She brushed a long strand of light-brown hair off her forehead and tucked it into the loose bun on top of her head.

"Why? Would you rather I stare at you?" Now that he mentioned it, that was a good idea.

Tori would know he was teasing. She got him, and their friendship by association had become a genuine bond. They spent a lot of time joking around, watching bad movies, and passing out in each other's guest bedrooms.

"I'm not doing anything worth watching," she said.

He looked her over again, this time lingering on her round hips, her full breasts, and her flushed lips. Sometimes he wondered if things would've been different if he'd met her before Riley. "I can wait for that to change, if you have something in mind."

Her shy smile shifted in an instant, and she ran her tongue over her bottom lip. She took a step closer. The shrill ring of her phone cut through the remaining space between them, and her hand flew to her hip.

Disappointment speared Archer's gut. "You're not really going to take a work call on a Saturday night, are you?"

"I have to." She grabbed two bottles of beer by their necks, spun on her toe, and wandered toward the back of the apartment, voice fading as she disappeared into Archer's guest room and closed the door behind her.

He shook his head in disgust and irritation. Most of it was directed at the people who worked for her. Some days he was surprised they didn't ask her to cut their food into tiny pieces, so they wouldn't choke. Part of the issue was she gave in without protest, but she saw it as *being a good manager.*

Archer pushed away from the island. He should join the party—be a good host and all that. He picked the farthest seat from Riley and Zane, which was maybe twelve feet.

It took focus, but he managed to keep his smile in place and the conversation flowing, as the next few hours wore on. Relief wormed its way through him as people stood to leave for the night, and over the next hour or so, his apartment emptied.

With any luck, this would be the last time he'd help an ex-girlfriend celebrate marrying someone else.

Riley pushed to her feet, tottering a little before she stood straight. Her grin was wide, but it had been for a while now. She grabbed one of her arms with her other hand. "Thanks for this. For all of it." Pink dotted her cheeks.

Zane stood behind her. As far as Archer had seen, he hadn't had a single drop that night. At least one of the two was sober, because Riley sure as hell wasn't. Zane rested a hand at the small of her back, expression neutral.

Riley opened her mouth again. "I'm—"

Zane whispered something in her ear. Her flush deepened, and she turned her gaze from Archer. "Nothing. Thanks again."

"Yeah. No problem." What were the odds the three of them could ever go back to the way things used to be, before the infinite number of times Archer and Riley dated, and the failed marriage proposal? When they were all happy being friends?

That past didn't seem to be in his future. Within a few moments, Riley and Zane were gone, along with the rest of the guests.

"That wasn't awkward at all." Tori's voice startled him.

He whirled to find her sitting on the counter in the kitchen again, kicking her legs back and forth.

"The work phone call or the Riley thing?"

"Either. Both. Can we not talk about work?"

Right. Because he'd tell her she needed to stand up for herself and make her people do their jobs, and she'd get pissed at him. Not irritating her sounded pretty good. "I mean it when I say I'm over her. It's… What if I make the same mistake again?"

She knocked back another swallow of beer and then wobbled in her seat on the counter for a moment before righting herself. She hadn't been this drunk when she took the call.

"How many beers did you have while you were gone?"

"Two or three. How many did I take with me? Here's the thing about Zane. He's arrogant, fickle, bossy, possessive, and has always been in love with Riley." She looked Archer over, something in her gaze burrowing past his surface. She laughed. "The two of you actually have a lot in common. Except he made it work in his favor."

Her words dug deep, until they collided with something he couldn't identify. "Your point is?"

She set her bottle aside. The glass clanged against the granite top, but nothing sloshed inside. "I'm sorry. It's true, you boys have a few less-than desirable traits in common, but for the most part, you're pretty different. Everyone can see that. Who knows what made the two of them work? I sure don't. Maybe Zane's a better kisser."

Knowing she was drunk didn't stop his pride from stumbling again. His ego was going to be limping into an emergency room if she kept this up. "I kiss fine."

"I'm not saying that's the issue. It's one option. It's not like I've ever kissed either of you."

"Even if I have no idea why they make a good couple, I'm pretty sure kissing isn't at the top of the list. There's nothing wrong with the way I kiss."

"Prove it." Tori straightened, some of the fog evaporating from her expression.

Archer raised his brows. He was wounded enough to be baited into the challenge. Besides, her full lips enticed him, and he'd wondered what kind of kisser—among other things—Tori was, on more than one occasion. Except this wasn't the time to find out. "You're drunk."

"I'm not propositioning you, and you're not taking advantage of me." The slur faded from her voice. "I'm saying you're not allowed to be the judge of your own kissing skills. If you're so sure that's not the issue… Or maybe you're not as certain as you act."

The taunt wasn't what pushed aside the last of his restraint, but it helped. The thing that broke him was the way she caught her lip between her bottom teeth. And the heave of her chest. And the way her posture highlighted every curve.

He closed the distance between them and rested a hand on her hip. Her shirt had risen, leaving part of her waist exposed, and her skin was warm and soft against his palm. He brushed a strand of hair off her forehead, and a pleasant jolt ran through him. Tori tilted her head closer. Her brown eyes were wide and dark, almost black in the dim light, and he couldn't look away.

He settled his other palm at the back of her neck, holding her head steady, and pressed his lips to hers. His blood roared in response. She whimpered and parted her lips, and he darted his tongue into her mouth, to dance with hers.

How have we not tried this before? He wasn't sure where the thought came from, but he let it linger. He pressed between her legs. Her fingers dug into his chest, hot even through his shirt. Every time she touched him, his pulse increased another notch. She locked her knees around his waist, and a low groan tore from his throat.

They broke apart, both of them gasping. Her cheeks were bright red, and she danced her fingers over her swollen lips.

"Yeah, the kissing isn't the problem." Her voice was breathy.

She hopped to the floor and draped her arms around his neck. When she rubbed her body against him, his cock throbbed. He backed her against the counter, diving into another kiss when she pressed her lips to his again. He should pull away. She was drunk. Didn't know what she was doing.

She raked her nails up his back, sending another wave of want through him.

Then again, it felt like she knew exactly what she was doing.

A loud *bang* tore through the room, and they both jumped.

Tori's hand flew to her chest. "Holy shit."

A car backfiring. That was all. But that wasn't the reason his pulse raced. Reason seeped back into his thoughts. Tori's giggles were punctuated by short pauses, before the laughter won out again. Cool air rushed in around him, soothing his heated skin but not easing the strain of his erection against his zipper.

He nestled a hand on the small of her back. "You need some sleep."

"I'm fine." But it took her several seconds to stand straight.

He steered her toward the guest bedroom. "Come on."

She flopped onto the mattress and tilted to the side before sitting upright. It was a good thing they'd stopped. She was already going to regret enough in the morning, hangover-wise. He knelt at her feet, pulled off her socks and shoes, and set them by the bed. Part of him wanted to help her out of the rest of her clothes, but that would be a bad idea.

She tugged him to his feet. "You were always too good for her, you know."

The words cut deeper than any others she'd spoken tonight, erasing the last of his lingering arousal. Unable to reply, he shook his head, helped her lie down, and then pulled the blanket over her. She snapped her eyes shut the moment her head hit the pillow, and seconds later, steady breathing was the only sound in the room.

What the hell was wrong with him?

chapter two

Tori forced her jaw to work overtime, in order to pry her mouth open. She licked her lips a few times. It felt like she'd eaten her pillow in her sleep. And then the throbbing started, pounding behind her eyes and inside her skull, and rolling into her gut.

She breathed deep, to calm the nausea. A familiar scent greeted her, brushing a layer of calm over her body's roaring protest of consciousness. What was that? She sat up, and her skull threatened to spin off. Why was it so dark? Oh, right. She opened her eyes and winced, as they adjusted to the light filtering through the blinds. She didn't have blinds in her bedroom.

She managed to focus enough, to look around the room. Which wasn't hers. More reason permeated her aching brain. Archer's guest bedroom. Right. She brought her fingers to her lips, as the night before plummeted in on top of her hangover. She remembered the kiss. Wow, did she remember it.

And she remembered why she'd been drinking so much. Work had been an absolute nightmare at nine on a Saturday night. She glanced at the clock, and the hammering in her head grew another notch.

Could she leave her skull behind? She'd woken up in the bed of the guy she'd thrown herself at, and if she didn't get back to her computer soon, work would be even worse come Monday morning.

At least her shoes were easy to find. She'd file that under *Small Things to be Grateful for*. As she pulled her socks on, a new smell assaulted her. Not as delicious as the pillow she'd woken up on, but it called to her stomach, causing a grumble in response. Bacon. It was almost enough to push aside her embarrassment for the way she'd behaved last night and definitely enough to draw her from the room.

Not that she could hide out in his guest bedroom forever, anyway. She dragged her feet across the area rug and then scuffed them along the hardwood. *What am I going to say to him?*

She hesitated at the edge of the hallway and watched his back as he cooked. When she let herself linger on the idea, she could admit he was attractive. Strawberry-blond hair just brushed his ears, and when he faced her, his hazel eyes drilled into her thoughts.

He was nearly a foot taller than her five-four, and years of hauling around boxes of comics gave him a narrow waist and shoulders almost broad enough to fill a doorframe. And since he owned the comic-book shop on the main floor of the remodeled Victorian where his apartment sat, he pretty much hauled those boxes around full time.

"Hey." He hovered the frying pan over a plate when she stepped into the room, his smile casual. "Breakfast?"

It wasn't unusual for him to make her breakfast, or vice versa. She couldn't count the number of times they'd stayed up all night, watching movies at one of their houses, then waking up in the same place they'd passed out.

"Um, sure." Sometimes she felt bad her contribution tended to be oatmeal and fresh fruit, but she managed to push the concern aside now. There was no reason to ruin an experience as delicious as the pancakes he was making with something like guilt.

His friendly greeting erased some of her hesitation. Were they pretending nothing happened? She wouldn't be able to live with the stress of that.

She dropped into one of the empty stools on the opposite side of the island from Archer, and he slid a plate in front of her—bacon, pancakes, and scrambled eggs instead of over-easy. That made her smile. Runny eggs were gross, and nobody ever remembered she didn't like them. *Except Archer.* Her stomach wouldn't have been able to handle the sight this morning.

"Dig in," he said.

She poked at her eggs, trying to find the right words.

"Is something wrong? You're suddenly vegetarian or something?"

"About what happened last night." She forced the words out before she could have second thoughts.

Archer paused with a bite of pancake halfway between the plate and his face. He put his fork down, the corner of his mouth tugging up. "That was a lot of fun. I mean, not all of it, but the bit I suspect you're talking about."

"But was it... I mean... Are we...?" What was

she trying to say?

"Eat something, before it gets cold." He nudged her plate closer. "It was a kiss, and it was amazing, but it wasn't like we fucked. I'm fine with it, if you are."

Was she relieved or the tiniest bit disappointed that he brushed it off so easily? She needed to focus on the relief. If there was one thing life had taught her, it was that getting involved with a guy recovering from a breakup was worse than *seppuku*—ritual suicide.

She chalked up half of her reaction to misplaced ego and nibbled on a piece of bacon. Her disappointment that he dismissed the kiss had nothing to do with how good he tasted last night. His hands sliding over her. The way he wore his T-shirt and sweat shorts this morning—she took a bite of pancake—or that he made a world-class breakfast. "I'm good with it," she said.

There. That sounded sincere, right?

The corners of his eyes dropped for the slightest moment, before his smile returned full force. "Awesome. You sticking around or coming back for anime club?"

He let the community-college anime club hold screenings in his comic shop on Sunday afternoons. He claimed it was because they bought things, so it was good for business. She suspected it was because he'd been a member once, and he knew how much they struggled to find club venues. A loud, familiar buzzing hummed through the room, and Tori's gut sank. She knew that sound all too well—sometimes she imagined she heard it in the middle of the night, and she woke up in a cold sweat, waiting for it to happen again.

Archer grabbed the phone from the counter behind him and handed it to her. "It's been going off all morning."

Shit. She shouldn't have let herself get distracted. "I can't do club stuff today," she told him as she clicked on the phone. "This is Tori," she said into the receiver.

"There's still a problem with the art. Have you checked the email I sent yet?" Candace's voice was frantic.

Tori bit back a sarcastic, *Good morning to you, too.* That would only make things worse. "I haven't had a chance yet. I just woke up."

Across from her, Archer leaned against the far counter, arms crossed and lips pursed.

She turned away from the disappointment in his hazel eyes. "I'm bringing it up now." Her lie emerged without hesitation. It would be true soon enough, anyway.

"Shoot me a note as soon as you know. I need to drop it with FedEx"—a harsh edge ran through Candace's pleading—"and let manufacturing know to expect it."

More unspoken retorts died in the back of Tori's throat. Things like, *If you'd done your job on Friday, they'd already have it,* and, *If you'd done your job last night, we wouldn't be scrambling now.* She took another swallow of juice and counted to three before replying, "Stand by. I'll have an answer for you soon."

Tori was the Senior Vice President of Design for

her brother's cosplay-themed lingerie company. She hadn't wanted a management position—tried to tell Brad they'd both be happier if she stayed in her artistic corner and came up with new outfits all day. He insisted they were business partners, and her job should reflect how important she was to the company.

Except Tori sucked at disciplining her people. She knew she had a problem, but not how to fix it. Most of the time Candace was amazing at her job, so Tori kept her on, but the one thing Candace excelled at was leaving her work until the last minute, which meant Tori rushed along with her to meet their deadlines.

Tori stood and started to thank Archer for pancakes and to apologize for not being able to finish.

"Sit down." He cut her off before she could say a word.

"I can't. I have to take care of this. I'm really sorry. I know you worked hard on breakfast."

"I don't care about the food. It's eight on a Sunday morning. It's not fair they expect this of you. It's not right that you put up with it."

Same argument as always. And she'd never be able to make him see she'd rather do the extra work and get it done, than tear into a talented person over habits they'd never change. "I don't *put up with it*; it's my company." She couldn't keep the irritation out of her voice.

"Brad doesn't keep the same kind of hours you do. Tell me he puts up with shit like this, and I'll drop it."

Sometimes she got so sick of Archer acting like he knew what was best for her, when all it did was add to her anxiety. "Brad has his own problems, and puts up with his own crap. That's why we've got two different jobs."

"That's not what I'm saying, and you know it."

With her hangover, she wasn't prepared to ignore an assault on both fronts, and something inside snapped. "I do, and you're not getting it. We can't all work for ourselves and own our perfect business, in a house we inherited from a loved one. Some of us have to put up with the real world and a large-scale mess, and sometimes that means putting up with other people's bullshit."

He clenched his jaw. "Don't get mad at me, because they don't treat you with respect and you refuse to deal with it."

The calm tone tugged her frustration loose, and tears pricked her eyelids. She choked back a snarl of frustration and stormed toward the front door, not trusting herself to speak. He was supposed to be her friend. He was supposed to understand why she had to do this. He wasn't supposed to throw it back in her face.

Tori paced between her couch and coffee table, careful not to trip over her laptop's power cable. She should be working in her office, but she was already pissed off about having to work over the weekend, and there was no way she was sequestering herself while she blew her Sunday, making sure every last line on a pair of *Inu Yasha* panties fell in the right place.

When Tori and Brad started the business, it was

supposed to be for kicks. She never expected it to turn into an on-call twenty-four-seven kind of thing. Over time, she helped a random employee here and there, never able to walk away when her people struggled. And one day she woke up and realized work consumed most her life.

When they started this whole thing, she loved the work, but covering for everyone else burned her out. The only advantage to the job these days was Tori got to do it from home. She often considered quitting, but the idea still meant so much to her, and she couldn't let Brad down like that.

Her newest line of lingerie was designed on an exclusive contract with a national chain, which meant the retailer had enough cash to sue for every missed deadline, and the non-stop emails from Legal never let Tori forget it. Meeting their timelines shouldn't have been a big deal. Candace simply had to check the newest design art on Friday, drop it in the FedEx box by close of business, and it would be at its destination Monday morning.

Then Candace missed the Friday drop, and when she checked the patterns Saturday night—a task she should have done a week ago—there were mistakes. Tori tried to talk her through corrections at Archer's, and Candace said she got it. Apparently that wasn't the case.

But it would be fine. As long as the client had the new art before Monday morning. Tori started the download, to grab the illustrator files off the office network, then leaned back on the sofa, staring at the ceiling. Her headache had faded, and that was something, but the memories of the kiss with Archer taunted her. She hadn't felt anything like the spark they shared, even with—

She pushed the thought aside. Now was the wrong time to relive the past. Not that she'd ever come across a good time for it.

She turned her attention back to her work laptop. What had gone wrong? Why didn't the layout look right?

And then she saw it. Candace's last job before the weekend had been to convert the file to the client's preferred format, but the image Tori saw was skewed and would only make panties to fit a paper doll. Because Candace had chosen the wrong file type on save.

Fury and frustration pumped through Tori. She closed her eyes and took a few calming breaths. At least it was a quick fix. She typed out a quick e-mail to Candace, explaining the situation and the error. She scanned it three times before clicking *Send*. It read politely.

She turned her attention back to checking the re-saved image. So far, it looked good. A whisper of relief flitted through her. Maybe her entire Sunday wouldn't be lost after all.

About thirty minutes later, her e-mail pinged. A response from Candace. Tori's gut sank to her feet when she saw the message. It couldn't be a good sign Legal had been copied, and Brad was on there too. He didn't need to deal with this.

Tori's irritation mingled with resurging rage and helplessness as she read the note.

I saved the file exactly the way you trained me to. If it wasn't right, it's because you missed a step in your instructions.

Tori's hands shook, as she typed out a reply. She couldn't think clearly enough to make it sweet and passive, so she settled for, *We'll revisit your training on Monday. I need to meet this deadline.*

She tried to make her frustration evaporate as the day wore on. Each new success lightened her mood, but every time, it was squashed by another message from Legal, demanding a reassurance that the Monday morning deadline would be met.

And the text from Brad—*You need help?*—did the opposite of what he probably intended.

Tori sent back a terse, *I'm on it, thanks*, then immediately felt bad about her reaction.

By the time Tori shut off her computer at eleven thirty in the evening, her eyes watered, either from staring at a screen all day or with the looming tears of frustration. Really, the only thing she knew was she spent most of her day correcting a mistake that wasn't hers and putting together a plan of action no one else was going to follow, which barely left her time to fix the original issue. The artwork had to be sent digitally in the end, and there would be a fine for not providing a hard-copy, per the contract, but it was better than dealing with another lawsuit threat.

She flopped back on her bed. The last thing she thought before she drifted off was, *Maybe I can get Archer to teach me how to talk back.*

Right. Like I could ever do that.

chapter three

Archer leaned forward on the glass counter next to the register and rested his forearms on the aluminum frame. He was careful not to smudge the glass. A stack of receipts lay in front of him for the various ingredients he used to make *onigiri*—rice balls—and bean-paste filled buns. He needed to tone back the treats for the anime club meetings. Sure, it was a tax write-off, since they were a community-college club. And if he was honest with himself, he enjoyed hosting them for weekly screenings.

The problem came down to money; it wasn't flowing in the comic shop as it had in the past. The club members weren't buying like they used to, and he didn't know if he could afford the added expense much longer.

He sank onto a stool behind him. He was bummed Tori hadn't been able to make it. Again. He might have been worried the kiss scared her off, but he knew she spent the entire day working. He desperately wished he could get her to take a stand with the people who worked for her. Point out that screw-ups wouldn't be tolerated, instead of fixing the problems for them. But she insisted it was better not to rock the boat.

Wishing wouldn't solve anything with Tori. He needed to concentrate on business. If he got his latest project off the ground, he wouldn't need to tell the anime club to find a different place to hang out on the weekends. Charging them for the snacks didn't feel right. He turned his attention back to his laptop, eyes glazing over when he looked at the search-engine optimization information again. The website was his attempt to bring in business on a national scale. He had to get his name on the radar, and he didn't have a lot of money left, so he was pecking through the process himself.

Tori offered to have her future sister-in-law look at it for him. She insisted Gwen was a genius at this stuff. Archer couldn't ask something like that, though. Not for free, and not from a friend of a friend.

Fortunately, he'd picked up enough from Zane over the years that he knew his way around most of the back-end technology. *Zane*. Archer's mood dropped another notch.

A bell chimed, drawing him out of his plummeting mood, and he looked at the door. He pushed a smile onto his face for the distributor from his favorite independent comic company. "Hey, man."

Archer liked Elliot. The guy didn't give him crap about his order numbers being down, he had a sense of humor, and he never seemed to know if he dressed the salesman or the fanboy part. He tended to wear all black—the universal uniform of the geek who didn't want to put time into their wardrobe—but instead of T-shirts and tattered jeans, he donned more professional corduroy slacks and button-down shirts.

Elliot lounged against a nearby wooden back-stock rack. "I'll put you down for five hundred copies of our next month's releases?"

Even when things had been good, he couldn't have moved that many issues. "Sure. And toss in a thousand action figures, too."

"So what have you been up to?" Elliot asked.

They bullshitted for a couple of hours, and as the sun vanished behind the mountains, Archer realized he needed to close up soon. He tried not to acknowledge that no one else had come in the shop during Elliot's visit.

A familiar car pulled up out front. Tori had broken free of her self-imposed shackles for the night. That was a bright spot. He turned back to the conversation. Why did seeing her make him so happy? Tori stopped by all the time, and it had never before put this kind of smile on his face.

Then again, he'd never before had memories like those of the kiss, to draw from and expand on. The way her body molded to his. The soft, hungry swell of her lips. Her moans.

And that was a couple of kisses. Since Saturday, his imagination treated him to what it would be like to strip off her clothes, taste her smooth skin…

He pushed the thought away before it could make his cock any harder, and forced his attention back to business. The bell on the door chimed again, and Elliot looked up, pupils dilating when he saw Tori.

Archer bit back an unwelcome rush of jealousy.

Heavy circles hung under Tori's eyes, but her

smile was genuine when she looked at him. She held up a dry-cleaning bag, wrapped around what looked like red velvet. "Someone is supposed to come looking for this tomorrow."

When Tori wasn't babysitting the assholes who didn't respect her, she designed and made custom costumes. She occasionally took commissions from Archer's clients. If he remembered right, this was supposed to be a recreation of an outfit seen on one of those pseudo-historical dramas on cable. *The Tudors*, maybe?

He nodded behind him at a closet rod he'd suspended from the ceiling for her. "You know where it goes."

She stepped around him, and her shoulder brushed his back. A jolt ran through him. That felt nice. Damn. What was wrong with him? Too long since he got laid, or something.

Seconds later, she took her spot on the stool across from him. He almost gave her crap about working too hard, but he wasn't in the mood to be snapped at. Instead he settled for, "We missed you yesterday afternoon."

"Trust me, I would've rather been here. I mean, that's normally the case, but especially yesterday."

An ache echoed through his knuckles, and he realized he'd clenched his hands into fists. He flexed his fingers until the blood flow returned to normal.

"This is beautiful work." Elliot leaned over the counter to examine the dress, and rubbed a bottom corner of the hem between his fingers. "Really gorgeous. Have you ever thought about doing this full time?"

"Technically, I do."

Except with the custom work, she got to pick and choose which outfits to make, instead of bowing to the whim of some underwear store. Working a little harder, to make ends meet, had to be better than the shit she put up with. It wouldn't do Archer any good to say anything, though. She'd resent him for it and then close off, instead of actually dealing with the problem.

The conversation slid from one topic to the next, until Elliot checked his phone. "Whoa. I love chatting with you guys, but I have to be in Denver tomorrow, and I've got an early flight out. I'll catch you later." He looked at Tori. "Seriously, you need to do more of the costume thing."

A new surge of jealousy tore through Archer, and he pushed it back. "She absolutely should. Catch you later, man."

He almost—but not quite—felt bad for rushing Elliot out the door and locking it behind him, but it had been a long day.

He turned back to Tori, who'd moved from her spot on the stool and leaned against the glass, watching him with an unreadable expression. The stretch showed off how well her jeans hugged her hips, and drew his eye to the Nintendo logo across her chest.

"You sure you're allowed to be away from work for so long?" he asked.

"I think they'll survive tonight." Even as she answered, she checked her phone again, the way she had every five minutes since she'd arrived.

He wished her reassurance matched her actions.

"You're sure?" He kept his tone light. "You're not convincing me."

She gave a half-laugh, half-sigh and pocketed her phone. "I can't help it."

Inspiration struck. He shouldn't indulge the thought, but it wasn't going to leave him alone unless he did. "Maybe I'm not distracting enough. If I kissed you again, could I hold your attention a little longer?"

"I—…" She fiddled with her fingers, not quite meeting his gaze. "It was really good, don't get me wrong, but I'm sorry I teased you. And even if it was amazing, and even though I like hanging out with you, I don't like you that way, and I don't—"

He placed two fingers over her lips, to stop the babbling. "It's okay. Really. We went over this yesterday morning. A kiss is just a kiss. Sex is just sex. I'm not asking you to mar—" the words *marry me* died on his lips. Why had he gone down that path? He had a different goal in mind. "To go out with me."

She was blushing, and standing right in front of him. "How do you do that?"

"How do I… tease you?"

She laughed, and it sounded more natural this time. "Joke about sex, like it doesn't mean anything."

"It doesn't. Or rather it has some meaning, and it can be amazing when it's done right, but there doesn't have to be any love attached to it."

She shifted her weight from one foot to the other. The pink in her cheeks faded, but her lips were still flushed and tempting. "You sound like Jen."

"Can we not talk about my sister and sex in the same conversation?" He adored his sister—usually.

But that didn't mean he wanted to think about her now.

"Sorry. But seriously, I don't know how you can say it doesn't mean anything. Sex and love go hand in hand."

"They don't for me." He didn't know why he was beating his head into this brick wall. Tori didn't think the same way, and he wasn't going to convince her otherwise. But something—either stubbornness or the insistent throb of his cock—compelled him to keep talking. "Sure, you *can* have both. You don't *have* to have both."

"I get what you're saying, but if it's not... That is..."

Archer dug through his head for an appropriate response. This was one conversation he didn't need her withdrawing from. "If your reason is you wouldn't do it *just because*, then I'm cool with that. But if you're thinking something specific, it doesn't do either of us any good for you to not say it."

"Since the sex isn't that great even when I'm with someone I actually love, I can't imagine it would be worth the trouble if there wasn't an emotional connection." She chewed on the inside of her cheek as she watched her shoes trace lines on the concrete.

He hadn't expected that. Knowing her assumption was based on a past of bad sex made any response die before it surfaced. He considered his words carefully, still very much wanting to have the conversation and having no desire to piss her off. He couldn't completely ignore the part of him hoping to change her mind. "It may not be emotion so much, as the other person involved."

His confidence grew when she tilted her head to the side instead of scowling or storming away, and he continued. "And it may not have been him. It may have been you weren't compatible with whomever. Different people have different kinks, and just because you find someone who's got similar sexual preferences, doesn't mean you have to love them. It simply gives you both a chance to get off, no strings attached."

"You make it sound so simple."

Damn, her shy flush was hot. He tried to push back his growing arousal and failed. "Finding the right buttons isn't always so simple. The rest of it? It absolutely is. At least for me."

"But— How do you know you're both going to like it? Especially if you're not dating."

After the kiss the other night, he was pretty certain he'd enjoy it. And his experience told him Tori simply needed the right motivation to let loose. "You don't know for certain, any more than you know how a relationship is going to go when you first start dating. Sometimes it's incredible and there are fireworks, and sometimes… not so much."

chapter four

"I guess I get that." Heat—both frustration and arousal—flooded Tori. "My brain doesn't work like that, though. I sleep with a guy because I love him."

"Your choice, definitely." Archer hovered a few inches away, towering over her, his crossed arms accentuating broad shoulders, and the corner of his mouth pulled up in a smile. "I'm not trying to convert you, but you sounded curious about how the other half thinks."

"I want to understand." She should drop the subject or change it, or something. But the desire pulsing under her skin wasn't convinced walking away was the right decision.

"I don't know any other way to explain it. Short of a hands-on demonstration, I'm tapped for ideas."

"So show me." Her skin flared red-hot at the thought of his hands running over her in any sort of demonstration. Despite her protest moments earlier, now the idea was in her head it refused to relocate.

"You're serious?"

"Unless you're not interested," she said. Given how close he stood, he had to be interested. "And the point is that it's only physical, right? Teach me, oh wise one.”

"You're sure?" He settled a hand on her hip, and studied her face.

She was anything but sure. But the slick warmth between her legs was positive. "Yes."

"It's easy. We already know we don't like each other *like that*, right?" He dipped his head, lips brushing the outside of her ear, and his voice a whisper.

She knew that as much as she knew anything—she wasn't interested in anyone who was on the rebound. "Right." Her voice came out softer than she intended, and she winced.

He slid his lips along her jaw. "So, you keep that in mind as we progress into the physical." He pressed his mouth to hers, the feather-light sensation sending sparks through her. She rose on her toes, to get closer, and he rested a hand at the small of her back. She parted her lips, and his tongue danced in and around hers. She dug her fingers into the defined muscles on his chest.

Every inch of her body was like a live wire when he pulled away. A dark look tempered his teasing. "We're not madly in love now, right?" His voice had dropped half an octave.

"Right." It was true. She still didn't have any desire to commit herself to him, but she did want something else.

"And no one gets hurt if we keep going."

She licked her lips. She wanted another taste. More than a taste. "Exactly."

"Because here's the thing." He glided his mouth down her neck. "I know I said the kiss the other day was nothing"—he nipped at her shoulder—"but I can't stop thinking about every single detail, and I'm real curious to see what else we can get up to."

Each touch branded new images into her thoughts. In her limited experience, no other man's voice sent electric tendrils through her, and she ached to discover what else he could do. "I'm game."

It was as if those two words broke some kind of rein. His gentle touch vanished, and his low growl rolled through her. He tangled his fingers in her hair, tugged her head back, and crushed his lips to hers. She whimpered at the sudden hunger. She wanted to be closer. To feel more. To taste him completely.

"You really don't usually enjoy sex?" He guided her back until her butt collided with the glass case near the register.

Oh, sure. He picked that out of everything she'd said. "Sometimes."

He trailed a finger down her spine, and she arched her back at the light touch. "I'm not sure if you've set the bar too high, or if everyone else has been that bad." His voice was low, but firm.

He didn't have anything to worry about so far, and they'd only kissed. When he pushed up the bottom of her shirt, a groan escaped her throat. With calloused fingers, he caressed the sensitive skin along her waist. She forced out a response. "It'll be fine."

"I don't want *fine*." He nipped her earlobe, mouth hot and demanding against her skin. "I want every moan and gasp to be sincere." He shoved her shirt higher and ran his thumb along her stomach. "Tell me what I have to do to make you scream."

A new rush of apprehension flooded her. Or was that arousal? She couldn't describe her desires out loud. "More of the same?"

"Hmm…" He danced his lips over the hollow at the base of her throat. "I guess we could do this all night. I was looking for something more specific and hoping for something more… graphic."

He teased the bottom of her breast through her bra, and she leaned her head back, inhaling sharply at the seductive touch.

"You like that?" He traced his tongue up her collarbone.

She wanted his mouth lower. Wanted fewer clothes between them. She nodded.

"So tell me."

"I can't." But the thought wasn't as terrifying as she expected. Her blood pounded in her ears, and an insistent pulse raced under her skin. Every inch of her begged for attention.

He dropped his hand to her waist and moved his mouth to her ear again. "If you can't say it, I won't know you're enjoying it."

"Play with my nipples." The words came out breathier than she'd intended, and speaking them made her heart thump faster. The need between her legs pleaded louder for attention.

He raised his mouth to hers and kissed her with intense hunger. With his fingers, he sought out the hard nub under her bra, caressed, and teased through the lace. Each time he crossed the rigid peak, a spike of pleasure tugged at her.

"Harder."

He pinched the swollen flesh, tugging and

rolling it between his fingers. She moaned at the sensation, as it stole the oxygen from her head, leaving her brain feeling like it was full of helium. They should go somewhere more private. Someplace that wasn't a corner of his showroom. What if someone outside saw? Caught a glimpse of them through bookshelves in the dark room?

Instead of terrifying her, the possibility added to her arousal. Being part of an unintentional peep show made her even wetter. Driven by the combination of Archer's touch and her new thoughts, she unclasped her bra. Her breasts tumbled loose as the tension binding them loosened.

She pushed out her next request. "Use your mouth?"

He shoved her shirt and bra out of the way and lowered his head. She gasped when he wrapped lips around her nipple. The sound seemed to spur him on. He flicked his tongue over the sensitive region, his teeth occasionally scraping her skin. She swayed her hips with each tug and lick. He blew lightly on the damp skin, sending a pleasant chill through her. He cupped her breast, thumb continuing where his tongue had left off, as he moved his head to the other side.

With his hand lavishing attention on one fleshy mound and his mouth worshiping the other, the ache of want from her sex became impossible to ignore. She tangled her fingers in his hair and held him to her chest, but it wasn't enough. She dropped her hand to his waist and then lower. Her surprised *oh* mingled with his groan when she traced the bulge through his jeans. "So big." The words slipped out before she could consider them.

He shifted his weight against her, grinding into her touch. She caressed his cock through the denim, images of him pushing inside her dancing in her head and taunting her.

A flash of headlights passed over the window, before vanishing and leaving the room dark again. Tori's pulse threatened to tear loose from her veins.

He moved his mouth back to hers, his hand still working. Then he broke the kiss and frowned. Her hammering heart skipped and tripped.

"No condoms." His voice was heavy with disappointment.

"Don't move." Every inch of her protested when she broke away from him.

She could almost feel his gaze tracing her figure, as she bent over the glass, to grab her purse from under the counter. It didn't quite make up for the loss of his touch, but it did short-circuit her brain in other ways. She liked the idea of being watched.

She plucked a condom from a side pocket and twirled back to face him.

"Do I want to know why…?" he said.

"The things you learn in college. My sorority sisters got more out of the spare I carried than I did, but since someone was using it, the habit never died."

"Makes sense." He grasped her fingers between his and led her toward the other side of the room and the tables and folding chairs his paper-and-pencil and figurine gamers used. He dropped into one of the seats and turned her to face him.

He settled his hands on her butt, and he pulled her closer until she stood between his legs. The interruption fled to the back of her mind, as she sank into the moment again. He traced his fingertips across the edge of her waistband, until he reached the button in the front. He laid a line of soft kisses along her stomach, as he undid her jeans. The combination of light and aggressive touches flooded her with a drive for more. She tugged her shirt and bra off, and then bent at the waist.

He didn't wait for her to ask this time, before he flicked his tongue out over a hard nipple and then wrapped his lips around it. He crawled his hands over her hips, pushing her panties out of the way and brushing her ass on the way down. His words vibrated against her breast when he spoke. "Tell me what you want."

"More."

"More what?"

He was going to make her say it, and she realized the only thing bothering her was that she wanted to speak the words. This wasn't her.

But apparently it was.

"Finger me." The two words rolled off her tongue and made her clit pulse.

He nipped her skin with his teeth, pushed her upright, and shoved the rest of her clothes to the floor. "I love the way that sounds."

She kicked her clothing aside. Heat flooded her skin when he looked her over, his gaze appraising and pupils wide.

One hand on her hip, he tugged her back to him. When he parted her lower lips with his fingers and brushed her swollen sex, a sharp gasp tore from her throat. He flicked over her clit, and sparks of pleasure shot through her. Waves rocked her body as he increased the pressure and speed of his attention.

She moved against him, the sensation leaving her light-headed. Tiny moans echoed from her throat each time he bumped her clit. His pace increased, and she whimpered at the rush tearing through her.

He moved his free hand to her leg, and glided his thumb down her inner thigh. The light feeling catapulted her over the edge. She pressed into his hand as she came, grinded on his fingers as the climax washed over her, and then pulled away when the touch became too much.

Her legs wobbled, and she reached out, to steady herself on his shoulders. She was too lost in the moment, to care about what she should or shouldn't be saying. "I want you inside me."

He unzipped and rose enough to free himself from his jeans, but didn't take them off, before dropping back into the chair, and then turned her away from him. She heard the tear of foil, and seconds later, he led her back into him, his hands on her hips. He glided the head of his cock along her slit and nudged her aching opening, and she dropped down slowly, gasping as he slid deep inside her, stretching her.

He set the pace as she bounced against his thrusts. Another orgasm built. As they found their rhythm, he sought out her breast, and pinched and tugged in time with his thrusts.

"I'm so close." She liked the sound of the words rolling of her tongue.

With his other hand, he followed the tender skin along her pelvis until he found her clit. He traced light circles around the still-tender area and moved his mouth along her spine and to the base of her neck. "Come for me." His words caressed her skin

He dug his teeth into her shoulder as her bounces became more of a grind. Climax tore through her. She rode the sensation, clenching her pussy around his cock. His grunts grew punctuated, and he lay hungry kisses across her bare back. He pushed harder against her, almost frantically, and then, with one final groan, slowed to a stop.

She pulled his hands to her stomach and leaned back. His shirt was rough against her skin, and his heart hammered through her back, competing with her own. As they struggled to find their breath, he softened and pulled out of her.

"I don't think anything that filthy has ever come out of my mouth." She settled her head against his chest.

"That was definitely sexy, but I wouldn't call it filthy. Riley says worse things than that every day."

An unwelcome pain shot through her. She winced and jerked away. No attachment. Right. And that was why.

"Sorry." His voice was soft in the dark room.

She grabbed her clothes and yanked them on as quickly as she could without tripping. "No worries. I need to get home anyway."

Apparently he was wrong. There had been a lot of love in that act, just not between them. It wasn't so hot to have a third person in the room, after all. At least not Riley's ghost.

chapter five

Archer shuffled down the street, head down, and hands shoved in his pockets. He'd gone for a walk, hoping to clear his head. He couldn't make his mind focus on any one topic long enough for him to figure out a solution, so his thoughts swirled with concerns he didn't have answers for.

He'd have to rearrange some of his orders for the month, to pay his power bill. There was no way around it. But what about next month? Or the month after?

And then, there was Tori. Who, given everything else, should be at the bottom of his worry list. She was at the forefront of his mind—the incredible night with her, her voice, her pleas, and the fact that with one little verbal slip she'd been gone. He hadn't seen her for over a week, and she ignored his texts.

He could stop by her house, but if she was working—and there was a ninety-nine percent chance of that—it would be easy for her to tell him she didn't have time. He shouldn't have pushed her the other day, but she said she was okay with the no-strings sex. A bitter laugh rolled through him. He should've known better. She was so closed off. Why would this be any different?

Is it possible this doesn't all fall on her? The question nagged him. All right, so maybe mentioning Riley hadn't been the best idea. It wasn't as if he compared the two, though. And Riley had been the furthest thought from his mind when Tori sat naked in his lap.

The memory played through his head, temporarily distracting him. Middle of the street— not the best place for a hard-on. He needed to figure out how to get Tori to talk to him again. *Maybe start with an apology?* And he needed to stop talking to himself.

A familiar voice caught his attention. Great. Now he was hearing Tori. He looked anyway, and there she was, a little ways down the street, outside her future sister-in-law's diner. On the phone. Go figure.

Whoever she was talking to—guessing wasn't difficult; it would be someone from work—had her pacing, gaze on the ground and upper lip pulled in a sneer.

Even engulfed in a heavy cloud of irritation, she looked incredible. She'd tied her long hair back into a bun and held it in place with a pen. The squares on her Tetris T-shirt seemed strategically placed, to draw the eye to her chest.

She hung up, a scowl marring her face, and then headed inside without seeing him.

This was an opportunity to clear the air. And next month's power bill hadn't come yet, so he had a little more time to find a solution to that particular problem. He pushed into Gwen's diner. Even in a crowded dining room, it only took a second to spot Tori at a table in a back corner, checking her phone every few seconds.

He dropped onto the bench across from her. "Come here often?"

She let out a tiny squeak and looked up. "Holy shit. You scared me."

"Sorry." He tried to mean it. He hadn't wanted to startle her, and he had to force his hand to stay by his side instead of brushing over her red cheeks. "We haven't talked in a while, so I wanted to say *hi*."

"I know. I've been—"

"Busy. Right." He'd expected that. "But you've got a few minutes now?"

"I had to drop off fabric samples for Gwen's dress, and she's making me sit and eat, but I have to get back to work soon."

Of course she did. He didn't want to push her into an uncomfortable situation, but they had to have this conversation.

"She's doing me a favor, so lunch is on me," Gwen said from behind him. "You want to toss anything on her ticket?"

He wasn't so broke he couldn't afford to feed himself. He didn't need charity. *It's a genuine offer.* It didn't matter. The logic couldn't squash the whisper of envy that Gwen could afford to do things like give away free meals, while he struggled to pay utilities. "Water. I don't know if I'm staying."

"One cheeseburger, extra cheddar." Gwen spun away.

Apparently, he was predictable. Another day he

might put up a valiant front and argue, but right now, he'd rather be talking to Tori. Who continued to glance at her phone every few seconds.

He reached across the table and covered her hand with his. "Be honest with me?" It was the only thing he could think of to say.

"Of course."

That had been too quick. Too easy. But he'd take it for now. "Either we move past this, or we stop speaking for good." He winced at the bitter taste of the ultimatum, but he wasn't going to play a game of *nothing's wrong*, when something obviously was.

"It's nothing." Again her answer came too fast. "I've been busy."

"Right. I'm sorry about what I said. I wasn't trying to compare—" He cut himself off. No reason to make the same mistake. "I wanted you to know the other night was incredible, and I kind of screwed it up."

"Kind of?"

"You know I enjoy your company, right?"

"I… Yes? I assume, since you haven't ever told me to fuck off."

Some of his tension evaporated. The joke, though it bordered on self-effacing, meant she was listening.

"Speaking of fucking, we're not going to let this hang over us, are we?" he asked.

She ducked her head and fiddled with her phone, but instead of checking it, she spun it on the table with her finger.

"Tell me what you're thinking. I know you can. You didn't have a problem saying what you wanted the other night," he said.

Her face went as red as the vinyl benches they sat on. "That was different."

"Order up." Gwen slid their plates onto the table. She glanced between the two of them, and then clucked. "And, I'll leave you two alone."

Archer might have thanked her, but she was already gone. He gave his attention back to Tori. "It's not different. If you didn't enjoy the sex, then it is what it is."

Her head shot up. "No, that's definitely not an issue. It was… wow."

"So do you accept my apology?"

"I don't know how to act around you now."

He pushed his food aside and leaned forward, resting his weight on his forearms. "Avoiding me probably isn't the way to go. Act however you're comfortable, but I was hoping nothing else would change."

Maybe a couple of things would change. For instance, he'd spend most of his free time, and some of his not-so-free time, fantasizing about the husky voice she used when turned on. About how she let loose. How she felt, wrapped around him. Saying so probably wouldn't help the situation.

"So we act like nothing happened?" she asked.

"Definitely not. It happened, and I'm not forgetting it anytime soon. But nothing else has changed."

"Once again, you make it sound so easy."

He nudged her shoe with his. "And you're making me think I'm wrong. Tell me we're good, but only if you mean it."

"We're good. I mean it."

A tension he hadn't realized was there drained from his neck. "When can we do it again?"

"You're horrible. I'll check my calendar."

That was natural. The kind of joking he could handle. "I'm glad you broke away from work for a little bit today. I didn't think you ever left your cave between five and five on a weekday."

"I had to get out for some fresh air. But I was actually serious when I said I didn't have long." As if to emphasize her point, she checked her phone again.

This needed to stop. He grabbed it and tucked it into his pocket. "They have to let you eat." He pushed her food toward her. "Keep me company, in the process."

She opened her mouth but shook her head without saying anything. She took a bite of her sandwich, chewed, and washed it down with tea, before responding. "I probably shouldn't ask this, since it tends to be a mood killer, so tell me if it's an off-limits topic."

"Nothing's off limits with me." He hid a cringe the moment the words were past his lips. She wanted to ask something about Riley. Maybe one thing was. Too late to take it back, and he'd pushed her. He couldn't justify holding anything back at the moment.

"Why did she turn you down? When you proposed?"

The question tugged at an avalanche of unpleasant memories he tried to repress on a regular basis. He wanted to spit out the easy answer. Maybe a defensive, *Like I know*, or, *Because of reasons*. Instead, he found himself spilling the truth. "She and

I didn't want the same things for our futures." And apparently, she'd always been in love with someone else.

"Like what?"

He raked his fingers through his hair. "I want kids. I want a wife to help me raise them, and a woman who wants to be taken care of—who takes care of me in return."

"I think that sounds sweet."

"But it obviously isn't for her."

"She figured out what was. I envy that." The longing in her voice dug deeper than Archer expected.

An awkward silence descended over them. This wasn't what he had in mind, when he said he wanted things back to normal.

"I should get back. Phone, please." Tori held out her hand.

Back to exhaustion. Back to the people who demanded too much of her. Back to burying herself in stress. He held the phone up between his thumb and forefinger, dangling it over her palm. "Take the afternoon off."

"Uh, no?"

He dropped the phone in her waiting hand. "Why not?"

"Because if I walk away and things break, I have to clean them up when I get back. And answer the e-mails that go along with them. And do damage control. And figure out who gets yelled at. I don't like yelling at people."

"If you're there, you'll do all of that anyway. You'll answer the same question fifty times and get the same one hundred e-mails. How much will change if you get their messages now or in eighteen hours? Send them a note. Tell them you have an emergency and you'll be out the rest of the afternoon."

"I can't." But she stayed in her seat.

"If you're looking for me to talk you into it, let's assume I already have. You pretend you argued valiantly, and let's declare me the winner of this debate."

Despite her heavy sigh, she didn't look upset. "All right. Just this once." She tapped something out on her phone and looked at him again. "Done. E-mail says I had an emergency and I'll be back later."

He couldn't hide his grin. He grabbed the device, turned it off, and dropped it into his pocket. "Perfect."

"But"—she reached for him and then dropped her hand—"I need that."

"I'll give it back later. You're taking the afternoon off; you don't need it until tomorrow morning." He stood and grasped her fingers between his.

"What if they try to get a hold of me?"

"Blame me. Tell them I wouldn't let you talk to them."

"That might not go over well."

He tugged her to her feet and her soft scent filled his nostrils. He closed his eyes and dipped his head to whisper, "They'll live without you until tomorrow morning."

chapter six

Tori stood at the top of the mountain, a cool breeze tearing strands of hair from the loose bun on her head. Archer was behind her in the short line, shoulder close enough to her back she felt his warmth, but he only occasionally brushed her. She tried to appreciate the gorgeous day, the surrounding peaks, and the canyons—snowless in the summer. The tangible electricity flowing between her and Archer made it difficult to think about anything except him.

At least she wasn't thinking about work. The word tugged at a diminished pit in her gut and brought her worry back full force. It would be okay. Archer was right. Nothing would happen she couldn't fix tomorrow. When she got her phone back, she had to expect countless e-mails from people who felt otherwise.

Besides, the warm, strong, attentive, and immediately-behind-her man was much more pleasant to focus on, especially combined with the memories of their night together. Heat raced through her, as the graphic images assaulted her. She needed to tone back the thoughts, or she risked spending the entire afternoon in damp panties.

"Your turn." He nudged her forward, hand at the small of her back. His palm seared her.

She inhaled sharply through her teeth.

"You okay? Second thoughts?" His concern was palpable.

Nope. She should be having them. *Skipping work. Sleeping with a guy I'm not dating.* But she wasn't having any, and that was the problem. It also wasn't what he meant. "I'm good," she said.

He wrapped his hand loosely around her upper arm. "Hold on."

"Hmm?" She eyed him, curiosity mingling with her focus on his warm palm against her skin. He reached a hand behind her and plucked out the pen holding her hair back. Her hair tumbled down and into her eyes, pale brown locks obscuring her vision. Her breath caught when he locked his gaze on hers. What was he doing? Was he going to kiss her? She realized she was licking her lips and stopped.

He shook his head and handed her the pen. "Pull it back up after. Trust me; it won't survive the trip down."

She stowed her whisper of disappointment there was no kiss, dropped into the steel-frame car, and tugged on the fabric restraints. Archer told her it was called an Alpine Coaster—like a roller coaster, but better. She might as well be sitting in a micro-sized dune buggy, attached to a pair of steel rails where the wheels should be. It was only big enough for her, and she wasn't sure how it was anything like he described. Something whirred, something else clicked, and the barely-a-car jerked forward.

She was towed higher and higher. She'd never been up in the Utah mountains before. She'd moved to Salt Lake City for her last year of college, to get away from her ex.

She pushed that part of the memory away, not wanting to ruin the day. Since she didn't ski and her friends thought the mountains were old news, she'd only seen the tops from an airplane seat.

The car reached the highest point on the track and paused. She looked around, taking in the view.

And then her thoughts and stomach dropped out behind her, as the car plummeted. The steel frame rocketed downhill and up again, through twists and turns, moved by momentum rather than a motor. It reached the top of another peak and teetered, before shooting down the other side. She screamed every time the gravity stole her gut, and she let herself be tossed back and forth as the cart carried her through the entire coaster.

She was laughing by the time she rolled to a stop at the bottom. She stumbled climbing out, and struggled to find her footing after repeatedly having her stability ripped away and the laws of physics forced on her in rapid succession. Somewhere in the midst of the chatter around her, she heard another car slide to a stop.

A pair of strong hands grasped her arms and helped her stand upright. "Steady." Archer's warm breath brushed her ear.

She wobbled a little more, using the excuse to lean back against him. She shouldn't. It didn't stop her.

Something new tickled her ear—she wasn't

sure if it was a growl or a sigh. "Having fun?"

What was she doing? Flirting with her one-night stand, who also happened to still be recovering from his last relationship?

She forced a neutral expression onto her face, pulled away, and faced him. "Absolutely." Her voice was too bright, but it was too late to take it back. "I can't believe I've never been up here before. If I ever get another day off work, this is the first place I'm headed."

"Call me if that happens."

"What's next?" She turned away, trying to focus on the lighthearted feeling of the day, instead of the desire his offer summoned.

He fell into step beside her, arm brushing hers as he nudged her in a new direction. "We go back to the top of the mountain, more slowly this time, stay a bit longer, and head down at not-quite breakneck speed."

"Okay…?"

There was no line this time. The ticket holder ushered them forward within seconds of their arrival. Archer gestured for her to go first, and she stepped hesitantly into the plastic box with windows, that was suspended from a cable.

"Gondola ride," he said, as he grabbed hold of a railing that ran around the inside of the car.

They swayed back and forth as they lifted from the ground, but their surface stabilized as it slowly rose up the side of the mountain. Trees and rocks passed by. It was all so pretty. He settled his hand on the small of her back, and she leaned into the gesture.

"Thanks for bringing me up here. I don't think

I've ever had a friend force me to take a break before. It's been nice."

"Never? What kind of friends are those? Next thing you're going to tell me is you've never had a guy bring you flowers."

A new kind of heat flooded her, and a sick ball sank in her stomach. She pulled her gaze from his.

"Oh." His tone was flat. "Really? Never?"

Wow. His disbelief didn't help her embarrassment. "My prom date bought me a carnation. It's no big deal, though. I'm not much of a rose person."

"That still doesn't make it right. What kind of flowers would you want?" With his thumb, he traced small circles along the base of her spine.

Not that it mattered. Still, it would be rude not to answer. "Daisies. I've always loved daises."

"I'll keep that in mind."

"So why do you get the afternoon off?" she asked after a couple of minutes of silence.

"Derrek is watching the shop."

His nearness compelled her to lean farther into him. His chest met her back, and he slid his hand to her hip. This was nice. She should pull away, but even though the thought was there, the desire wasn't. "Alone… on a Tuesday afternoon… in July? You're not worried about him getting overwhelmed?"

"I'm worried about a lot of things—and trust me when I say I wish that was one of them—but no. He'll be fine."

She wasn't sure what to make of the comment or the trace of bitterness running through it, so she didn't say anything. Instead, she honed in on the feeling of his heartbeat through her back.

He broke the silence again, a few moments later. "I'm thinking about asking the anime club to meet somewhere else on Sundays."

That drew her attention. She turned to face him, breath catching when his face was inches from hers. She could either back away or enjoy the nearness. She held her place, and her words fell out. "Something's going on. You love keeping them around."

The car jerked to a stop, and they both stumbled. He reached a hand out to steady her, and when they righted themselves, his lips hovered near hers. He finally stepped back, and disappointment washed over her as the air swept in to take his place.

"We should get off." His voice was heavy.

"Here?" Images flooded her head. Sex in a public place, suspended several feet over the mountains in a moving car, with the chance of any random person seeing them? The thought made her pulse race and a slick warmth spread between her thighs.

"We're at the top of the mountain. I didn't think you'd want to head back down right away."

"Right. No. Good call. Let's hang out here for a while." She pushed aside the graphic fantasy— mostly—and stepped past him onto solid ground.

Clusters of people gathered around different roped-off tour areas. She was relieved when Archer led her off the path, away from the crowds, and toward a quieter, cooler part of the mountaintop. The trees weren't dense—not like she was used to seeing back in southern Illinois, where she'd grown up—

but they provided enough of a canopy to keep the heat out and still let streams of sunlight through.

They walked in silence for a while, Archer with his hands shoved in his pockets, sometimes drifting closer and sometimes drifting away again. When he spoke, his voice blended with the surrounding scenery. "Anime club's not paying off the way it used to. It doesn't drive up sales anymore, and there's no point in letting them leech my back room if they're not buying anything."

"What's the real reason?" She wouldn't push under most circumstances, but he brought it up. She'd try to pry it out of him, and drop the subject if she couldn't.

He leaned back against a nearby tree, tilted his head toward the sky, and propped one foot on the trunk. They'd wandered a ways off the trail, and any voices were rare and distant. For minutes at a time, it felt like they were the only people in the world. The silence was pleasant. Too bad she couldn't bottle it for use later.

He finally looked at her. "The store isn't making as much money as has in the past. Most months we're breaking even, but it's why I didn't replace Sam when she left for college."

"But you always have people in there, and you sell a ton of comics."

The corner of his mouth quirked up, but the smile didn't reach his eyes. "Please don't take this the wrong way, but it's been a long time since you were around for more than about thirty minutes. I don't always have people in there. And they buy comics, if they buy anything. The collectibles, the figurines, the board games—those were what made the money. No one wants those anymore."

An ache of sympathy rolled through her. It wasn't supposed to be this way. The desire to help surged through her. She'd loan him the money, give it to him even, but he wouldn't take it. "You can do stuff to expand, right? Sell online—things like that?"

"I'm working on that."

The irritation in his voice caught her off guard. She found herself stepping back, and she crossed her arms. "All right. It was just a suggestion."

His expression softened, and he shoved away from the tree. "I'm sorry. I didn't mean to snap." He shoved his hair off his forehead. "I've got it under control. I needed to vent a little bit, is all."

She didn't want to delve into any issue that made him scowl or threatened the afternoon. Not that she wanted to pursue most issues anyway, but now there were extra reasons to change the subject.

His shoulders and neck relaxed, and he moved closer. He trailed a finger down her right arm, raising a trail of goose bumps. "I'm stressed about it, but I shouldn't take my frustration out on you. I'm having a lot of fun this afternoon. More than I think I've ever had up here."

"No big deal." The sun dropping toward the mountaintops, and the feather-light touches against her skin, were enough to chase away the residual tension over his reaction.

He pursed his lips before giving her a casual half smile. He grabbed her fingertips, tugged her arms loose, and pulled her with him when he leaned against the tree again.

She stopped less than a foot back, focusing on the friendly contact and the tingles it sent through her, tucking the awkward moment into the back of her thoughts.

"I've pretty much driven the entire afternoon. Anything you want to do while we're up here?" He rubbed his thumb over her knuckles.

An uninvited image popped into her head—an expanded version of the fantasy that teased her at the end of the gondola ride—and heat flooded her skin. Knowing that wasn't what he meant didn't make it easier to shove the graphic suggestions out of her brain.

It was a struggle to keep her voice steady and clear. "I hadn't really thought about it."

He raked his gaze over her, drawing more ideas to the front of her thoughts. Memories of the look in his eyes when she stood in front of him naked. Murmurs of the thrill she got from telling him what she wanted.

"Nothing at all? Because I'm open to suggestions," he said.

She shook her head, any response catching in her throat.

"That's too bad." He raised a hand to the side of her face and traced the outer edge of her ear. "I was hoping you might describe your wishes to me in vivid, excruciating detail." His voice dropped an octave.

She raised her head. The glint in his smile hadn't been there before. Was he thinking the same thing she was? *Take the chance.* "I might have something in mind."

chapter seven

"That is, if we're allowed to do this again." The shy current in Tori's voice was nullified by her proximity, which let Archer feel her heat.

He trailed a finger down her bare arm. "Why wouldn't we be?"

"You know—no strings. It didn't mean anything. Doesn't that mean no repeat performances?"

"We're not in love." The reply came out weaker than he intended, and he swallowed, to find his voice again. "But if we had fun, there's no rule that says we can't do it again."

"Out here?" She didn't look panicked or concerned. Instead, her smile moved in.

He made a show of looking around. "We're in the middle of nowhere. The closest voices are so far away, it doesn't matter. But"—he dipped his head and hovered his mouth near her ear—"if you tell me the idea of something so intimate happening in a public place makes your blood run cold, we'll leave."

"It does exactly the opposite."

He was really starting to adore this side of her. Daring. Less inhibited. "Is that a *yes*?"

"Just don't get us caught."

He skated his lips down her neck. "Unless whoever catches us wants to watch?"

Her laugh blended into a moan. She pulled his head to hers and kissed him. Her tongue traced over his bottom lip before sliding into his mouth to tumble and tease.

His cock pulsed and strained against his jeans. She tasted incredible. His body remembered what it felt like to be buried inside her, and it roared for another chance. But he still had enough sense to know stripping her down in public—isolated or not—wasn't the best idea. There were other things he could think of, though, as delicious and requiring the removal of far fewer clothes.

He spun, taking her with him, and pressed her back against a tree. He dropped a hand to her breast. When she moaned and ground her hip against his cock, it throbbed. Sometimes long, seductive hours of playing were nice, but this wasn't the time or place, and the way she stroked the bulge below his waist told him she agreed.

Every sound she made intoxicated him. When she spoke, her lips caressed his skin. "That feels good."

"That's the point." He wanted her to talk again. He hadn't said it right the other night; he'd never been able to get a woman to open up during sex the way she did, and hearing Tori say what she wanted poured fuel on his desire.

There was a pause, and then her reply reached out and grabbed him. "I'm so wet right now."

His dick strained painfully against its prison,

but it would have to wait. He dropped his palm along her stomach and dipped below the waistband of her jeans. "I want to see for myself." He hovered his mouth inches from her ear.

His reward were tiny mewls tearing from her throat, and a wide-eyed nod.

He undid her pants and then pushed under the elastic of her panties. Her heat greeted him, and her juices coated his fingers the moment he dipped between her folds. A guttural groan rumbled from him at the sensation, and his cock begged for a taste.

Her gasp told him the hard nub under his fingers was where he wanted to be. He framed her clit with two digits, and stroked.

As he rubbed faster, she closed her eyes and tilted her head back. Her moans came in small bursts. He rocked against her hand as she caressed his erection through his jeans. Her touch grew harder, more insistent, as his rhythm increased. She was stroking him now, as much as possible in this position. She bucked her hips and parted her lips.

Tori's, "I'm so close," was quiet, but he heard it. He was pretty sure he was about to burst as well.

He increased the pressure, rubbing her clit harder and faster. Her breathing hit the frantic pace he recognized from the other night—a noise that teased him in his dreams.

"Stick your fingers in me."

Oh, hell. He plunged his hand lower, palm still bumping her clit, and shoved two fingers in her tight opening. She arched her back against him, cry drifting up as she clenched around his fingers.

He slowed as she did, but the throb below his

waist was painful, and he had no idea what he was going to do about it. Fuck. This was a bad idea.

She opened her eyes and pulled away from his touch. He gently eased his hand out. He could almost hear his penis chanting for its chance.

"My turn," she whispered.

Before he could ask for clarification, she dropped to her knees. He swore his zipper sliding down was the loudest thing he'd ever heard. It took the last threads of his self-restraint not to let his groan echo off the trees, when she encased his shaft with her fingers and gently worked it free. His eyes rolled back in his head, as she glided her tongue up his length. His knees threatened to give out, when she took him in her mouth, and he had to secure one palm on the tree behind her, to keep his balance.

A light laugh vibrated from her throat and through his skin, as she bobbed her head up and down, flicking her tongue over his sensitive head every few seconds. He'd been close to coming before she started sucking on him, and there was no way he could hold out with her full lips wrapped around him. He tried to pull her away. "Tori, hon." His plea came in short gasps. "I won't last much longer."

Instead of discouraging her, the warning spurred her on. The delicious sounds she made rolled through his dick as she sucked in time to pumping him with her hand. Tension built in his lower gut, and he dug his fingers into the tree. He grunted as he came, thrusting against the back of her throat, pounding until he was spent, and then going a little longer.

She slowed when a shudder racked through

him, and she kissed and licked him clean as she pulled away.

He grabbed her upper arm and yanked her to her feet with desperation. He settled his hand at the small of her back and kissed her deeply. Was that himself he tasted on her lips? Holy fuck, she was incredible. He finally broke the kiss, and rested his forehead against hers.

"You didn't have to do that," he said.

"I know. But it was too tempting to pass up." *Impish.* That was the only word he could think, of to describe the smile she gave him, as she looked up at him through her lashes.

The voices that had stayed at a distance most of the afternoon drew close enough for Archer to make out words. He adjusted himself as best he could, shoved his cock back in his jeans, and straightened his clothes. He couldn't take his eyes off Tori, while she zipped up and combed her fingers through her hair.

She looked up, and met his gaze. Pink spread across her cheeks. "Should we head back down?"

"Can I buy you dinner?" He wrapped an arm around her waist and steered her toward the trail, stumbling a few times as his legs regained their sense of balance. He couldn't help but notice hers did something similar.

"Aren't you supposed to do that before, not after?"

He shook his head and pulled her closer. Okay, so maybe that wasn't appropriate, given their relationship—or lack thereof—but her curves yielded to his touch, and there would be plenty of time later to pull away. "I'm not always as traditional as I claim to be."

"I'm fine with that." She lay her head against his side and slipped her hand into his back pocket. "Dinner would be wonderful."

The ride home was quiet, but it didn't have the awkwardness Archer expected. It felt appropriate. Occasionally, he looked out the corner of his eye and caught Tori studying his profile, but she turned away quickly. He'd rather she spoke her mind, but he couldn't complain about the sight of the plump, fleshy swell of her kissable bottom lip, as she bit into it.

Best not to let the thought linger. No-strings sex was fine, but experience had taught him spending too much time living in memories created ties that were painful to sever.

They pulled up in front of Gwen's diner, next to Tori's car, and he put his vehicle in park. He reached across her for the glove compartment, and… did she lean into his touch? No, he had to be projecting. He grabbed her phone and sat up. "Thanks for playing along today."

She shifted her posture, as if she struggled to keep the corners of her mouth pulled up. She darted her eyes to the device in his hand. "I had a lot of fun. Thanks for making me walk away for a little while." Her hand twitched, and she rubbed the pad of her thumb over her middle and forefinger.

He couldn't hold back his sigh. Faster than he could blink, she'd jumped head first into the same anxiety he tried to make her forget. "Don't work too late?" He handed her the phone.

"I'll do what I have to." She powered it on the moment she had it in her grip, tapping her thumb against the edge while it loaded up.

With that, she was out of his car and heading toward her own, the sickly glow of her BlackBerry illuminating her skin, as she dropped into her driver seat. He watched for another minute or two as she started the engine, but she didn't drive away. She moved her lips, and she shook her head. A scowl spread across her face, and a second later, she raced her thumbs over the keypad.

No job could be worth that kind of stress. Why couldn't she tell them where to stick it?

He honked, to let her know he was leaving, but she didn't even look up, her lips moving as quickly as her thumbs, while she typed out replies to whatever had her brow creased.

At least Riley had never taken any shit from a job.

The moment the name passed through his mind, the lingering pleasantness of the day vanished. Fooling around with Tori was a temporary thing. He wasn't falling again, even for her. Which was why he wanted nothing more with Tori than they already had. He needed to remember that. Drill it deep into his thoughts and not let go of it. No matter how much fun he had with her or how good she tasted or how much he loved the sound of her moans.

chapter eight

Tori paused halfway up the walk to Archer's, to admire the view. Not the well-trimmed shrubs lining the path or the tulips growing under the window—she watched the show on the other side of the bay window, in the open space that had been a living room when the house was built, over one hundred years ago, but was now the main floor of his shop.

Every movement he made stretched or elongated a new group of muscles along his back, neck, and arms. He rearranged something under the counter while he talked to a girl, who seemed about fourteen or fifteen and as captivated by Archer as Tori was.

Tori had ignored the attraction for a long time, but it wouldn't hurt to watch. They'd cleared the air, they both knew they didn't like each other *like that*, and he really was nice to look at. Her schedule had kept them from getting together again since the escape to the mountains, almost a week ago, but they'd texted, and everything seemed cool between them. He was right; she really could do no-strings sex.

She stored the rambling thoughts and made her

way to the shop entrance. The bell on the door chimed in greeting. She'd always thought that was a nice touch. A deceptively low-tech device, in a room wired with hidden cameras and alarms.

Archer looked up at the sound, and his customer took the excuse to study him again. Tori couldn't help but smile. Poor girl had no idea that even if she were ten years older, he was so far from interested in a relationship, it wasn't funny. An unfamiliar ache throbbed in Tori's chest, and she ignored it.

He nodded her over. "I'm surprised you broke free of the house-arrest bracelet."

"Why are you on house arrest?" The teenager's eyes grew wide, and she finally looked at Tori, taking a step back as she did.

Tori twisted her mouth to the side. How was she supposed to respond to that?

Archer laughed. "I'm teasing her, because she works too hard."

"Oh." The girl didn't look convinced. She continued to eye Tori warily, while leaning closer to Archer.

"This is Mara. Trigun."

Mara cleared her throat—an exaggerated sound. "*Sexy* Trigun."

Of course. Because a red, desert-and-battle-torn trench coat was a sexy thing. Tori was there to take measurements for that custom-costume order. She gave Mara a closer look. Close-cropped blonde hair, with streaks of pink. She was maybe an inch or two taller than Tori and had a slender build. Well, she had the body to pull the look off.

Tori extended her hand. "I'm Tori."

Mara hesitated before returning the handshake. "And you make all the cosplays people wear?"

"I make a lot of them."

"But have you done something like this before?"

Tori didn't flinch under the scrutiny. She'd done sexy vampires, sexy zombies, and sexy androids. "Not specifically."

"How do you plan to do this??"

Tori expected the question and welcomed it. It was a lot easier to work on a costume when the idea wasn't fully formed in the client's mind. Those who had a very specific image of what they wanted were usually disappointed by things like how gravity impacted clothing. Fortunately, Archer had warned her upfront what outfit was being requested, so she'd had time to think on the way over. "A fitted short skirt, strategically placed bandages on the chest, with a hidden zipper in back and a battered coat that hangs open enough to tease, but not enough to show anything inappropriate."

Mara's posture relaxed. She glanced at Archer. "What do you think?"

"I think you should trust the talented seamstress."

"But do you think I'll look good?"

"You'll look fantastic." Maybe Tori had misjudged her age. Maybe she was closer to thirteen or fourteen. Mara didn't look at her, but instead kept her attention focused on Archer.

He shrugged. "Tori's the best. If she says it will look good, you'll knock the right guy's eyeballs out."

"Awesome. You need measurements, right?"

Mara grinned, gripped the bottom of her T-shirt, and lifted.

Tori rested a hand on Mara's, to keep her from stripping in the middle of the store. Archer's, "Whoa," overlapped with Tori's, "Let's maybe do this somewhere… not in front of the window."

The words passed her lips and tugged a memory with them, searing her skin and making her pulse race. She met Archer's gaze, and he raised an eyebrow, a smile playing on his face.

Fortunately, Mara had already turned away with an exaggerated, "I guess."

A few minutes later, down-payment in pocket, and girl assured again she'd look sexy, Tori emerged from the back room. Normally she didn't have to be so precise with measurements, but for something as fitted as what Mara wanted, she'd need to know exactly how tight she could make the fake bandages.

Mara practically skipped out the front door, waving to Archer and promising to be back soon— just to visit. Archer's *goodbye* wave was stiff, and his smile off. At least he had the good sense to be embarrassed about a young girl hitting on him.

And then Tori noticed someone else was there. She was surprised to see Elliot. "I know it hasn't been a month since you were in here last."

"Actually, I was looking for you." He rubbed the back of his head, not meeting her gaze. "I'm in town to talk to someone else, and I saw your car out front."

He knew which car was hers? Something slapped against the glass counter, echoing through the room and startling her. She whirled toward the sound.

"Sorry." Archer gave an apologetic shrug as he shifted a pile of books into a neat stack.

"No worries." She turned back to Elliot. "What's up?"

He jammed his hands in his pockets. "I was wondering if you'd have dinner with me tonight."

"I… uh…" She snapped her jaw shut to keep it from dropping open. She hadn't expected this. Did she think of Elliot as *dating material*? She resisted the urge to look at Archer; it wasn't as if they were a couple. No strings, he was still rebounding from Riley, and all that. Instead, she tried to be subtle about looking over Elliot. She'd never noticed before, but he was kind of cute. Curious brown eyes hid behind his horn-rimmed glasses, and straight black hair accentuated his slender face.

Shit. She was taking too long to respond. There was no reason not to go, right? "Sure." She focused on making her smile genuine. "Sounds great."

A loud *bang* bounced off the walls, followed by the clatter of glass, metal, and plastic, striking glass. She jumped and whirled to face Archer again. He was kneeling next to the display case, and half the things inside had tumbled and fallen on top of each other.

"Oops." His expression was as flat as his voice.

Was he reacting to the conversation? She pushed the tiny voice aside. There was no reason to project her insecurities on him. At the most, he might be worried she'd sour things with his distributor. She'd make sure Elliot knew that whatever happened between them had nothing to do with Archer or his business.

♥♥♥

Tori picked at her chicken. She was having a lot of fun talking to Elliot, but with every passing moment, it became clearer why she'd been so surprised at the dinner invitation. There was zero spark between them.

He set his fork down without making a sound, pulled the cloth napkin from his knee, and fidgeted with it for a moment, before returning it to its spot. "If you two are a thing, you could have told me *no* without offending me. The truth would sting but I'd live."

For the second time that night, he'd caught her off guard. "I'm sorry, us two…?"

"You and Archer."

"We're not a thing."

"You're sure?" His brows rose past the tops of his glasses.

She was so sure, it ached. No. Wait. It didn't hurt at all. "I'm positive. Even if I were interested, he's still coping with what happened with Riley. Everyone knows that."

He snorted, then shook his head. "I'm sorry. I shouldn't find that amusing."

"It's okay, but I don't get the joke."

He leaned forward. "You've known them all for what? Four years?"

"Something like that."

"I've worked with Archer almost since he opened the place, eight years ago," Elliot said. "And I know a lot of people look at me and think *comic geek*, but no one survives this long in sales, without being able to read people at least a little bit."

"Okay…?"

"The whole twisted-love-triangle thing has been going on since before Zane enlisted. Between you and me, I'd bet my commission Archer means it when he says he's over Riley. He just hates that she was the one who left, and he's spinning his wheels, blaming himself for it."

"Archer's not like that."

He twisted his mouth in disbelief. "You spend more time with him than I do."

"Exactly." Was it true? No. It couldn't be. Not that it mattered; she wasn't interested anyway.

He turned his attention back to his half-eaten steak. "Speaking of Archer, since you and I obviously aren't going anywhere, give me an excuse to write dinner off instead?"

Her skin crawled at the implication. At least she knew now he had a different expectation at the end of dinner than she did. At this point, she was tempted to cut the conversation short and call a cab. He implied she led him on, gossiped about her friends, and then asked for a way get his money's worth for dinner if she wasn't putting out. "I can't make decisions on his behalf. I'm simply another customer."

"Right. Of course. But you're not. You're a brilliant costume designer."

If he hadn't already soured the evening, the compliment would have warmed her. "Thanks."

"And I still think you should be doing it full time."

"I already do." She was bordering on the edge of a mild confrontation, and she wasn't interested in that at all.

"Technically. Right. But here's the thing—we have a sponsorship option we're going to implement with different shops."

"How's that work then?"

"We don't ask for exclusivity or anything. Basically, we pay Archer and shops like his a set amount every month, and in return, he gives our books, posters—whatever we send him—high-visibility spots in his store."

Cool. Archer didn't like to ask for help, but this was payment for services, not charity. It sounded too easy, though. "That's neat and all, but how does it involve me?" she asked.

"I think the offer would be more valuable all around if we could loop you in."

"I'm sorry, I don't know what that means."

He chuckled. "It's easy. We'd ask you to provide a different outfit from one of our books every week—you pick the outfit, and we pay your standard rate—and it gets displayed in his shop. Sell it when the week is up. Do whatever you want with it. We'd pay him a little more, and you extra for your time as well."

Her heart jumped and her brain screamed that it sounded brilliant. A chance to do more of what she chose. "I don't know how that would be cost effective for you." Not what she meant to say. Damn it, her business oriented side kicked in.

"Trust me, the numbers work. All I need from you, besides the desire to do this, is to work whatever sexy magic you can on Archer, and get him to sign on as well."

Something about his tone and posture poured a layer of slime over her hope. She tried to shake the feeling, but it sank in. "I'll talk to Archer." As long as she could get past the way he reacted last time she tried to talk business with him. On top of that, could she suck him into something that didn't sit right with her to begin with?

"Right. Sure you will."

chapter nine

Ambivalence surged through Archer when Tori stepped into the shop. He couldn't believe he lost his cool last night, with Elliot around. And seeing her now—a hint of joy playing on her face and her posture relaxed—the unfamiliar jealousy danced with denial under his skin. Whatever was wrong with him, he needed to tone it back and get it under control. It was none of his business who Tori went out with.

He forced himself to smile. "Free of the chains, two days in a row? Is that a record?"

"Something like that." A waver ran through her laugh. She settled onto one of the wooden stools behind the counter resting her hands by her thighs on the seat.

He forced his attention to stay on her face. He wouldn't stare at her cleavage, the seductive curve of her breasts, and the way her narrow waist vanished into gorgeously grabable hips. He'd make small talk instead. "How was your date?"

"Not bad. Not fantastic, but you can't click with everyone, you know?"

A smattering of relief trickled through him.

Two boys, maybe eleven or twelve, wandered into the shop. Their shirts had an expensive designer's name on them, and their jeans sagged almost to their knees.

Both glared at him. The shorter one elbowed the taller one, whose upper lip pulled in a sneer. "What are you looking at?"

Great. A headache, and they probably wouldn't spend a dime. Archer shook his head and turned away. They weren't worth the grief. He'd let them talk their shit and leave when they realized the store was a troll-free zone. As long as no one else came in for them to bait in the meantime, it wouldn't be an issue.

"Damn straight." The snide retort hit his back. "Fucking pedo."

Archer clenched his teeth and turned to Tori again. He wouldn't react. He wouldn't pound the boys into a pulp, because it wouldn't solve anything, and more importantly, because he didn't want to deal with assault charges. It was half the reason he had the shop completely wired with cameras. Sure, it helped prevent theft, but the digital eye didn't lie in a civil case.

Tori twisted her mouth to the side, a new shadow falling over her eyes. If this level of confrontation was bugging him, it had to be devouring her. He was surprised she hadn't found an excuse to vanish into the back room. Maybe she was finally getting used to the fact that some people were just misery-spewing assholes.

"Anyway. What are you up to today?"

She leaned to the side, glanced at something

behind him, and then straightened again. "Not sure yet. I'm not used to having an entire free Saturday. If you weren't working, I'd say we should go do that Alpine Coaster thing again."

The flood of memories slammed back into him, bringing tastes and smells to tempt him. His cock twitched. Maybe if they found somewhere more secluded, they could get further than they had in the mountains. "Derrek's coming in at three."

Her smile grew, eyes pulling up at the corners, and then vanished when she looked over his shoulder again. "You can leave that at the counter until you're ready to pay." There was a waver to her voice.

Archer looked, to find the boys standing near the front door, the taller one's jeans not hanging as well as when they came in.

The shorter one whispered something. The taller one's sneer returned.

"I'm not carrying anything." His voice cracked, disrupting his lie.

Tori's arm brushed Archer's, as she moved to stand next him. A glance out of the corner of his eye told him her arms were crossed.

"The figurine you shoved down the leg of your pants. You need to pay for it." Her tone was firmer now. More clear and confident.

The taller kid took a step back and ran into the shorter one's hand. The taller kid said, "Fuck you, bitch. You can't accuse me of carrying shit so you have an excuse to make me drop my pants."

Archer clenched his jaw, and all the frustration from the night before rushed back, this time with a target. He crossed the room quickly, stopped short of the pair, and rose to full height. "The young lady said you've got something on you."

Shorty nudged his companion again, who mimicked Archer's arms-crossed-and-shoulders-back posture. The occasional crack in his voice would've been funny, if not for the words he spewed. "Your bitch doesn't belong in a comic book store. Why don't you leave us alone, you fucking pedo, and go find out what a real pussy feels like? Take the whore in the back room and rape her until she knows her place is in the fucking kitchen."

Archer wouldn't pound the kid into a pulp. Fists clenched, he uncrossed his arms and took another step forward. There was no reason to let the punk know he considered restraint.

Both kids stepped back at the abrupt threat, and a plastic-wrapped collectible dropped from the leg of the older one's pants and tumbled to the ground.

"Get out before I call the police and have your asses hauled to jail until you're old enough to buy booze." Archer spoke between clenched teeth, but his growl echoed back from the walls.

"Fucking pedophile. Feminist asshole," the kid said. This time, he ignored his friend's nudge and dragged him out the front door, occasionally glancing over his shoulder. His pace quickened when Archer took another step toward the door.

He wouldn't go after the kids. They weren't worth the hassle. Even if every bit of him wanted to pound their skulls until those boys learned respect. He grabbed the toy from the floor and raised an eyebrow when he realized it was one of his rare imports—a two-hundred-fifty dollar Japanese collectible.

He turned back to Tori, frowning when he saw her arms were still crossed, her fingers digging into her skin hard enough to leave pale marks. He set the toy aside and stepped closer to her. "Are you okay?"

She nodded, jaw clenched.

"You sure?" He caressed the back of her knuckles with his thumb.

"I'm fine." Her reply was raspy.

He pointed her back to the stool, grabbed a bottle of soda from the refrigerated case behind the counter, and twisted off the top before handing it to her. "Thanks for rescuing Nao."

"I didn't do it for her; I did it for you."

An impulse snaked through him, and he pushed aside the desire to dip his head and brush his lips over hers. Instead, he took a step back and leaned against the counter. "Then, double thank you."

♥♥♥

Tori shook the glass bottle, and the marble inside rattled around the bottom. The melon *ramune* Archer had pulled for her vanished half an hour ago, but watching the trinket inside kept her from thinking about the scene with the would-be shoplifters. Every time portions of the confrontation flitted through her thoughts, her gut churned.

Archer kept up more than his share of the conversation, occasionally asking if she was okay.

The door chimed, and out of instinct, Tori swiveled her head toward the noise. Out of the corner of her eye, she saw Archer do the same. It was Gwen, but not the woman who ran the diner down the street or dressed casually when Tori saw her with Brad. In her high heels, she was almost as tall as Archer. And they were nice heels. The matte black matched her slacks, and her white blouse hung like silk and didn't have a single wrinkle in it.

Looking past her, Tori saw a high-end SUV parked next to the curb outside, and the boys from earlier sat in the back seat, flipping Tori off from the rolled-down window.

"I always wondered what it looked like in here." Gwen swept her gaze around the room, lingering on a few spots, before giving Tori a quick smile and turning back to Archer. "I hear you met my charming nephews." She gestured at her clothes. "*I* dressed nice for lunch with my brother, but his kids are wearing jeans that sag past their asses."

Tori might have been confused by the almost cool demeanor but it was one of Brad's tricks. Give nothing away until the situation had been assessed. The question was, why did Gwen need to do that here? Why wasn't she profusely apologizing instead?

Archer stood up straight, hands at his sides, gaze never leaving Gwen's. "That's one way to describe them."

Tori wasn't sure she wanted to see whatever this was. Deep down, she wanted to hide in the back room until the conversation was over, but she sat frozen to the chair, afraid moving would draw unwanted attention.

"The older one—Robby—tells me you threatened him with physical violence"—Gwen's lips drew into a thin line—"and told him he was a worthless little punk and you were going to nail his ass to the wall.”

Tori coughed, and Gwen glanced in her direction before turning back to Archer.

“I’m sorry, that’s not the case. The boys were shoplifting. Tori stopped them. I threatened to call the cops on them, but no one touched anyone,” he said.

“Are you calling my nephew a liar?”

Tori’s confusion levels peaked. What the hell was going on? This woman, with those asshole kids as nephews, was about to marry her brother.

Archer’s Adam’s apple bobbed up and down, and his back went stiff. “You asked what happened, and I told you.”

“Because you’re making a serious accusation. Those darling angels”—her voice wavered then evened again—“have never been caught doing anything like what you say, and there are serious legal repercussions involved in making a claim like yours.”

Tori couldn’t do this. She knew Archer was going to stay as neutral as possible, and she knew his reasons, but this was different. She wasn’t going to let some snotty, stuck-up kid tattle after being an unforgivable ass and get away with it. She leaned over to the computer tied to the register, hit the right keys to exit the point-of-sale software, and then pulled up the directory with the security backups in it. She licked her lips. “Drop the bullshit act. This isn’t a business negotiation.”

“It could be. Prove otherwise.”

Nervous, sick adrenaline coursed through Tori.

"Did you see the sign when you walked in the store, saying we reserve the right to refuse service to anyone?"

"I did. I also saw the Better Business Bureau sign next to it. Have you dealt with formal complaints from them before?"

Tori swallowed a gulp of air, hands shaking against her knees. "Then I'm also certain you saw the signs warning that the shop is under twenty-four-hour surveillance and all interactions are recorded?"

"I did."

Tori turned the flat-screen monitor and started the footage from an hour ago. The abusive language echoed through the shop for the second time that day, and her gut threatened to evict its contents, but she swallowed back the sick and sat through the entire scene.

"Son of a bitch, you caught him." The edge was gone from Gwen's voice, replaced with something softer.

"Excuse me?"

Gwen dropped her purse on the counter, shoulders sinking. "I'm not stupid. I know the little fuckers aren't angels, and I know their father lets them get away with murder—well not literally. Not yet, anyway. They're deceptive, and they're good at what they do. Somewhere along the way, they learned how to spot cameras in shops and always keep out of view of them."

"Mine are well hidden." Archer hadn't relaxed.

Tori might not think much of Zane, but he was good at what he did, and that included wiring the comic shop with cameras no one could see and setting them to write the footage to a series of secure hard drives, with real time cloud backup.

Gwen glanced around the room. "I see that. Or rather, I don't. I'm impressed. I need to get the name of your guy—gal, whatever—and see if they can hook me up." She grabbed the cordless phone off the counter and handed it to Archer. "I'd like you to press charges."

"You would?"

"I wasn't trying to be a bitch. You're all but family. It's that the accusations have never stuck before, and it's too much hassle to deal with them if there's no proof." She nodded at the figurine on the counter. "If that price tag is correct, it's grand larceny. You have them on tape, they were shoplifting, and I know it's not my place to discipline them, but if their dad won't, I'd really like to teach them a lesson while they're still young enough to learn. Please, call the police. Press charges."

Archer was already dialing, before he talked to a dispatcher, and explained the situation.

Tori knew they still weren't getting the whole story. "So you know they're brats, and you let them wander down here alone? Did one of us piss you off?"

"I try to avoid places like this at all costs." Gwen's smile turned sheepish, the first crack in her exterior since she'd walked in, and pink peeked through her makeup.

Tori sat up straighter, indignation running through her again. "There's nothing wrong with this place."

"Except I would spend a small fortune on

Archer's figurines." Gwen's smile became a wide grin. "I love it in here. How do you not go broke in a place like this?"

The conversation lightened and continued to flow after Archer got off the phone. When the police showed up, they took Archer's statement, pulled Gwen aside, and eventually took the boys away in handcuffs in the back of their cruiser.

Derrek walked through the front door as the excitement wound down. "Did I miss something?"

Tori felt drained. The conversation with Gwen hadn't been bad, but the rest of the day had dragged her through the wringer, leaving her insides a crumpled mess.

"Not all that much." Archer looked at Tori, gaze softening with worry. "I'll explain later. Watch the shop for a few hours?"

"Sure."

Archer intertwined his fingers with Tori's and tugged her off the stool. "Come on." His voice was gentle. "Let's de-stress."

She didn't resist, as he pulled her up the stairs to his apartment. She was glad she didn't mind following him, because she'd used up all her arguments for the day. When they were inside, they both kicked their shoes off. He locked the door and then turned her so her back was to him.

He rested his hands on her shoulders and kneaded his thumbs softly into her neck. "You were brilliant today."

"I was terrified." She tilted her head forward, moaning at the gentle touch.

"But the important thing is you did it anyway."

She leaned into the attention, not sure how to respond. His lips brushed the back of her neck, and she gasped in pleasure and surprise.

"Sorry. I shouldn't have done that."

"You should have." She tilted her head to the side, to expose more of her neck. She'd switched off the filter which kept her from speaking her mind; part of her wasn't ready to activate it yet. Especially with other parts of her turned on by his touch and his skilled lips. "And you should do it again."

He glided his tongue up her skin until he met her ear, and nipped at the lobe with his teeth. "Have I ever told you how much I like it when you talk like that?" His whisper brushed her skin, sending a pleasant chill through her.

"It sounds familiar." She gave a light laugh, happy to sink into the moment and leave the rest of the day in the past. She reached behind her, grabbed his hand, and tugged him toward the living room. She pushed him onto the couch and straddled his legs. Draping her arms around his neck, she leaned forward and let her hair fall in a curtain around them.

There was still an element of terror involved with speaking her mind this way, but at the same time, it made her wet as hell. "Make me forget today, at least for a little while?" Her voice was quiet, but steady.

He grinned and rested his hands at the small of her back. He pressed his mouth to hers and then caught her bottom lip between his teeth, before pulling away. "Absolutely."

chapter ten

Every time Tori shifted in Archer's lap, his cock grew harder. Want rapidly replaced the adrenaline of the afternoon, making the throb between her legs ache for more.

Reason started to sink in, trying to tell her she shouldn't do this again. That this wasn't the way *no strings* worked. She ignored every protest. His sturdy legs under hers, his hard length pressing into her mound, and his hands sliding over her hips were enough to erase everything else.

He nudged her back, prompting her to stand, then pointed her toward the hallway. His hands never completely left her, and his chest pressed into her back when he rose. His lips brushed her ear. "We have time. Bedroom?"

She nodded and let herself be directed down the hall. She'd only been in Archer's room a few times, and the decor always caught her off guard. In contrast to the modern stainless steel and hardwood of the rest of his house, or the garish displays downstairs, this room was simple. Beige walls, dark sheets and furniture, and almost no other decoration.

Unlike everywhere else, it looked like no one

wanted to be there. And she knew he really only used the place to sleep. The almost somber feeling tugged at something sad inside. His lips running up the back of her neck chased away the crawling gloom.

She leaned back into him with a tiny sigh, as he glided his palms under her shirt and up her stomach.

She tilted her head to one side, to give him easier access, as he kissed along her shoulder. He traced his tongue along the curve where her neck met her back, and she gasped. She didn't know what to ask for first. Every inch of her was alive and begging for more attention.

He didn't wait for her to decide. He fumbled with her bra for a moment, before unsnapping it and pulling it and her shirt over her head. The contact between them broke for a second, and when his bare chest met her shoulder blades, she knew he was losing clothes as fast as she was.

He glided his hands to her breasts. When he grazed her rock-hard nipples, she whimpered and rested the back of her head against his chest. "Harder."

He obliged on two fronts, sucking on the sensitive skin of her neck, teeth scraping her shoulder, and at the same time, rolling her nipples between his fingers, pinching, and tugging. Pricks of pain rolled through her at the pressure, pooling between her legs.

She squeezed her legs together, grinding her butt against him as he tweaked, pulled, and sucked. Could she come like this?

Disappointment flooded her when all the attention stopped abruptly.

"I know I've been asking you to drive things." His hot breath chased across her skin, and he hooked his thumbs in the waistband of her jeans. "But I'm going to make a request."

Her pulse screamed in her ears, and her sex pleaded for attention. "Okay."

"I want to watch you play with yourself. I want to see you make yourself come"—he pressed his hard shaft into her ass—"and I want to stroke off while I watch."

She thought it was impossible to be more turned on, but the request dialed up her arousal another notch. "All right."

He pushed the rest of her clothing to the floor, and his knee met the back of hers, nudging her forward.

She stepped out of the discarded pants and turned to face him. He raked his gaze over her as he finished stripping. His cock sprung loose, standing at attention. Damn. That was hot.

She drew her hands down her sides, gasping as her body begged for more contact. She didn't remember a time her skin had been so sensitive. Her pussy ached when he took his dick in his hand and dropped into a nearby chair.

She backed up to the bed and took a seat. What was she supposed to do now? She closed her eyes, threw her head back, and wandered her hands.

She moved one to her breast, following Archer's path from earlier. His groan filled the room, mingling with hers when she found the hardened nub and squeezed.

She grabbed two of his pillows and positioned

them behind her. She lay back, shoulder blades cradled, and propped one foot on the edge of the mattress, dangling the other over the side.

She roamed her free hand down her stomach, spurred on by his, "God, Tori."

She brushed her outer lips with her fingers, sliding easily over the already slick surface. She dipped inside her folds, trying to stretch out the moment. Stroking everywhere but her aching clit. His grunts made her wetter.

"Do you like that?" The words slipped past her lips without thought, and she realized she liked the sound of them.

"Fuck, yes."

"Do you want me to come for you?"

"Yes, baby. Finger your pussy. Come for me. Hard."

She moved her fingers higher, moaning when she found her throbbing sex. "I'm so wet." She stroked the hard nub, panting disrupting her voice.

She didn't expect to peak so quickly, but the sensations, combined with the dirty talk, had her climax building inside. "I'm so close."

"Stroke yourself faster." An edge lined his voice. "I want you to make yourself scream."

There was no choice there. She rubbed her clit, still pinching her nipple with her other hand, and an orgasm tore through her. A cry wrenched from her throat, growing louder with shock and pleasure when he gripped her hips and shoved his cock inside her at the height of the moment.

Her yell melded into a series of whimpers, as he stretched her. Her inner walls clenched around his shaft every time he slammed deep inside her.

She wrapped her legs around him, resting her feet on his ass cheeks, and held him close, rocking against him with every hard, pounding thrust.

His groans filled the room, and his rhythm shifted to staccato bursts. "I'm coming."

She pulled him closer with her legs, the edges of her orgasm finally sliding off. He let out one final roar, and the frantic pace stopped.

He rested his hands on either side of her head, kissing her deeply, tongue and lips hungry. She pressed back, still needing to be as close to him as possible. He finally collapsed on the mattress next to her.

They lay there for a moment, struggling to catch their breath.

His quiet, "Fuck," made her frown.

"What?" she asked, not liking the nervousness creeping inside.

"Forgot the condom."

She should be bothered—scared or something—by the news. She sought out his hand next to hers on the comforter and intertwined her fingers with his. "I'm clean. I'm on birth control. You're clean, too?"

"Absolutely."

"No worries, then."

Archer rolled onto his side and gathered Tori to his chest. He draped an arm over her hip and rested his forehead against the back of her head. Her steady heartbeat was soothing and helped bring his pulse back to a regular rate. "Do you have to get home?" he asked.

"I think my place will survive without me for a while." She snuggled tighter against him, and it tugged at something deep inside.

He shouldn't be grateful. He shouldn't even care. It had never bothered him when Riley had to take off. Then again, Riley usually moved in within the first few weeks of them dating.

Not that he and Tori were dating. This was a novelty. A woman, wrapped in his arms, who didn't expect to move in at the end of the week. This was the only reason holding Tori close and safe was comforting. Because there was no way in hell he was falling for her.

He needed to back off before it was too late. Before history repeated itself, she moved on, and he was left wondering why he'd gotten involved. A nagging in the back of his head insisted losing Tori would hurt more than anything he'd dealt with in the past.

Tomorrow. He'd work on backing off tomorrow.

Wasn't her pillow softer? Tori struggled with the thought, as her consciousness was dragged to the front of her mind. She inhaled deeply. She knew that scent. *Archer.* Did she pass out in his guest bedroom again? Her pillow shifted, and a soft moan rumbled through her ear. *It's not a pillow. It's Archer.* The pleasant thought warmed her.

Her eyes shot open, and she sat straight up as

the night before came rushing back. The tenderness, the soft kisses, and the falling asleep, not ever wanting to leave.

"You okay?" Archer peeled one eye open.

She pulled the sheets up in front of her. Not like being modest mattered; he'd already seen everything. The thought heated her skin and hardened her nipples. She forced neutrality onto her face. "I'm good."

Except she wasn't. Half of her wanted to curl up next to him again and fall back asleep, and the other half screamed full volume that she needed to walk away. Now. That she wasn't going to make the same mistake as she had with her last boyfriend, and that she wasn't—despite what the rest of her thought—falling hard for Archer.

He reached up, brushing her cheek with one finger when he tucked a strand of hair behind her ear, and then dropped his hand abruptly. A shadow crossed his face as he sat, and he scooted farther from her. "Good." A faint strain ran through his voice. "Breakfast?"

No. She needed to get home. To suppress... whatever this was.

Reason softened her panic. A month ago, she would have stayed for breakfast. This wasn't supposed to mean anything. She was projecting, because she thought sex had to mean love. That was all it was. The reassurance didn't completely convince her, but it was enough to keep her from bolting. "Breakfast sounds great."

Besides, he did make wicked-good pancakes.

She couldn't help but stare when he climbed out

of bed—let her gaze trace every line of definition down his back, over his ass and thighs—before he pulled on jeans and a T-shirt. She looked away when he faced her, but not before he caught her eye.

"I'll see you in the kitchen?" His voice held a tone she couldn't identify. Exhaustion? Hurt?

She didn't want to know. She nodded, not sure he was looking at her. "Sure. I'll be there in a minute."

She watched his legs and feet shuffle past her, and his footsteps paused. She held her breath, unsure what she was waiting for. A disappointment she couldn't name washed over her when the patter of feet resumed again. Seconds later the door latched shut.

This was so bad. What the hell was she doing? She needed to obliterate this stupid crush, before things fell apart.

chapter eleven

Tori followed Archer down the stairs, from his apartment to the comic shop. She had to focus on the familiar. Their feet on the restored wood, the sunlight striking the side of the building and filtering into the hallway… everything that would be there if she'd passed out, watching bad movies with him.

Her tension was almost gone, that was nice. Breakfast had been normal, as long as she ignored the awkward pauses and unidentifiable looks, and now she was going to hang out and help him do inventory, until the anime club screening that afternoon.

She dropped onto a stool behind the counter, unable to keep her gaze off him as he opened the blinds, unlocked the door, and turned over the *Open* sign in the window. The way he moved, every ripple of muscle as he worked, was a sight she'd never get tired of. She ducked her head and studied her nails when he looked at her.

"I'm thinking today might be the last day I do this." Disappointment lined his voice.

She stared at him with wide eyes. "You're serious?"

"I don't think I can afford to host them anymore. I don't know how it's possible, but things are getting tighter every week. This is between us, isn't it?"

"Of course. Always."

The bell on the front door chimed. Customers already. Had to be a good sign, right? Tori's smile froze when she saw Riley in the doorway. The blonde was in jeans and a T-shirt, same as always, but this wasn't the kind of shirt that hugged her torso and barely covered her waist. This was faded, had an Air Force logo on it, and hung down to her thighs. It had to be Zane's.

Riley's flat expression shifted to a huge grin when she saw Tori, and she skipped across the room, to wrap her in a hug.

"I'm so glad you're here," Riley whispered.

Tori returned the embrace, relaxing with the familiar greeting. "You're up early for a Sunday."

"Hey." Archer's greeting was hollow.

"Hey." Riley leaned back next to Tori, bookshelves behind her, glass counter between her and Archer. Her pleasant expression never changed. "I know I don't have any right to ask this, but I'm going to, anyway. I need a favor."

Tori couldn't ignore her relief at the stilted interaction. This was awkward, and it shouldn't make her happy, but it did.

Archer's, "Anything," came too quickly for her taste, though.

Riley crossed her arms and took a step closer to Tori. "Don't agree to it before you hear me out. I'm here because you're local, and you deserve the business. Nothing else."

"You know I don't charge. Not getting what you want at home?"

Heat and embarrassment flooded Tori, and she wasn't sure if it was for herself or the other people in the room. Her breakfast churned in her gut. Was he really hitting on Riley?

A low growl rumbled from Riley's throat, soft but distinct in the room. "Don't make me regret this. I'm looking for a place to hold my launch party." Riley had contracted a series of graphic novels, several months back.

"I completely forgot that was happening so soon. Are you excited?" Tori pushed aside the tension settling over the room.

"I'm terrified. And thrilled. And you have to see the swag they've got for me. Trading cards, bookmarks"—Riley's voice dropped in volume—"and this is totally top secret, but if the first few books do well, they're talking to a figurine manufacturer."

"No. Way." Tori clapped once, glee filling her chest. "So incredible."

"And I was hoping, if I asked really nicely, you might make me some cosplays, like the school uniforms the boys wear. I'll pay full price. No arguments. One for Zane, one for me, maybe a couple for you two?"

"I love that. Absolutely." Tori had no idea where she'd find the time, but she'd figure it out.

"Of course you can do it here." Archer hooked his thumbs in the pockets of his jeans. "We'll order pizza—The Pie or something nice like that—and I'll get it all set up."

"*We* don't have to worry about ordering pizza," Riley's tone was lightly sarcastic. "And The Pie? Really? Don't worry about breaking the cobwebs on your wallet or anything. I have a marketing budget. I'll make the arrangements."

Tori wanted to shrink back on her stool, at the spike of tension. Riley never had trouble speaking her mind, and sometimes it was a lot of fun to watch, but it had never been pleasant to see her clash with Archer.

And he was acting like an asshole. What the hell was wrong with him, alternating between hitting on her and trying to completely control the situation?

"Don't worry about it." Archer's tone was deceptively casual, a strong thread of command running through it. "Save your budget for something else."

What happened to money being tighter than ever? Tori's head throbbed.

"I said I've got it covered." Any pleasantry was gone from Riley's voice.

"Seriously, it's no big deal." Archer's straight posture and strained neck looked like it was becoming a very big deal.

Riley's snarl of frustration echoed through the shop. "Holy fuck—really? *Jesus.* I've been here for less than five minutes, and you're already pulling this shit?"

"You wanted a favor. I'm offering my help."

"Then help. Don't try to dominate the situation."

Archer narrowed his eyes. "I thought you got

off on that."

Riley clenched her jaw, and there was a pause before she replied, "This was a bad idea. Forget I was ever here." She turned away, each of her steps shaking the store, as she stalked toward the door.

Tori wasn't sure whether to congratulate Riley, storm out after her, or slap Archer.

"Lee, wait," he called to her retreating figure.

Tori ground her teeth at the pet name. This was why she didn't get involved with guys like him. At least he reminded her all on his own. Elliot had been so very wrong about how Archer felt about Riley.

Tori was on her feet in a second, pace brisk as she followed Riley's path out the front door.

God, she'd been so stupid. What had she been thinking? She'd go home and bury herself in the punishment of work, until she'd scored into her head what a bad idea it had been to sleep with Archer.

"*Tori*. Oh, come on." His pleas hit her back, and she let the door swing shut behind her.

Riley was fumbling with her keys when Tori reached their side-by-side cars. Riley looked up, blue eyes hard and flashing with fury. Her expression softened, and she nodded at Tori's chest. "I'm sorry, I didn't know. I…" She trailed off, furrowing her brow. "That makes this worse. I'm sorry."

Tori looked down. *Shit.* One of Archer's shirts. She hadn't noticed before now. Now all she wanted to do was burn it. She gave Riley a weak smile. "It's not your fault, but thanks."

"It kind of is. I wish… You know, I don't even know."

Tori shook her head, not wanting to have this

conversation or Riley's pity. "It was my mistake. Lesson learned. Good luck finding a release-party venue." She didn't wait to hear if Riley replied. She was in her car and peeling down the road seconds later.

♥♥♥

Archer winced at the squeal of tires out front, but not as hard as he had at the first set, when Tori had torn out on the pavement. Uneasiness thrummed through him. He needed to call Tori now or text her or go over to her house and beg forgiveness. An obnoxious voice in the back of his head insisted he did nothing wrong. That he'd been trying to help Riley out, and both women had overreacted.

If that was the case, why didn't he believe it? He leaned back against the counter, grinding his teeth, frustration pumping through him. He couldn't believe he'd fallen into the same old power struggle with Riley. It wasn't that he needed to be right, but something about her refusal to be wrong pushed all his buttons, and not in a good way.

But he wasn't worried about Riley. Tori's face kept popping into his head—the red-rimmed eyes, the tight lips, and the fury in every line on her forehead.

He had his phone out in a flash. He should've kept a tighter rein on his instincts. Some of his worst habits reared their heads around Riley. How had they lasted any amount of time as a couple, let alone tried it more than once?

And he'd never wanted to put Tori through that. He had to tell her. Even if she was probably still driving, he couldn't wait. He sent her a series of texts.

I'm sorry.

Come back, please?

You'll miss anime club.

He hesitated, his thumbs over the touch screen, and he stopped himself from typing out, *I'll miss you.* There was no reason to dive so far in. Was there?

If that was the case, why was there a giant aching wound in his soul from the entire situation?

chapter twelve

Archer smiled, and his chest lightened for the first time in days, when Tori's car pulled up in front of the shop. She tugged a dry-cleaning-bag-wrapped something out of her backseat and trudged up the walk. She hadn't returned any of his messages, and she refused to answer the door when he showed up to apologize in person.

It took all his restraint not to run out, scoop her up, and kiss her, telling her how sorry he was. He wasn't sure where the compulsion came from, but everything about it appealed to him. Feeling her warm body against his. Tasting her. Making her moan.

She pushed inside, and her icy stare obliterated his impulse. Her gait was stilted as she crossed the room and draped the costume on the counter. "For Mara." She set a folded T-shirt next to it—one of his. "For you."

"Thanks." He poured as much warmth and sincerity into the single word as he could. "Can you hang out for a while?"

"No."

"Are you coming back later?" He hated the

desperation in his voice, but he needed her to hear it. To know he meant it.

"No." Her phone buzzed and was in her hand in a flash. Her tone turned pleasant. "This is Tori."

She reached the front door and spun on her heel, pacing toward the other side of the room again. She focused her gaze on the carpet for the most part. As she talked, she wore a virtual ditch in the middle of the floor. Her voice shifted from polite phone-voice, to abrupt, and then to the same clipped language she'd used with Archer. He'd heard her half of these conversations more times than he cared to count, but something was different about this one.

The pit in his chest grew, the more her mood soured, and every time he saw the tight lines on her face and her hard-set eyes, he beat back the desire to take the phone from her and tell off the person on the other end.

"Give me fifteen minutes." Her voice sounded like a blade, cutting through the air-conditioning. She dropped the phone in its holster and finally met his gaze. Her lips moved, but no sound came out. Red rimmed her eyes. She shook her head and turned away, the door rattling behind her seconds later.

He clenched his fists into tight balls. He'd never wanted to find someone and rip them a new one more than he did right then. Whoever had been on the other end of the phone should suffer for whatever they put her through.

At the very least, he wanted to wrap her in his arms and hold her until she knew it was okay. He would've given anything to be able to erase those lines off her face and soothe her nerves.

She wasn't talking to him, she wasn't dealing with things at work as they deteriorated, and he was powerless to do anything about it. Or maybe he could do something, and if it put even a little smile on Tori's face, he'd do it again and again.

He clicked on the first website his search engine directed him to. He picked out something with daisies, roses, and a teddy bear, and then paid for the as-fast-as-you-can delivery. He furrowed his brow when the screen told him there was a problem processing his payment. He tried again, and then a third time.

What the hell?

He took a detour to his credit-card site, and all sorts of negative emotions pumped through him when he saw the card was over its limit. How the fuck had that happened? He clicked back to the flower site, gave them his debit-card number instead, and then returned to the maxed-out balance.

How had he missed that? Things were worse than he realized. He needed a new money solution. Now. Maybe trying to puzzle through it would take his mind off Tori.

♥♥♥

Tori paced the length of her living room. The faded carpet scratched at her bare feet. She needed to get the crap replaced. Or maybe put down some throw rugs, like Archer's. Thinking of him added another layer to her mounting irritation. Best to ignore it and focus on the task at hand.

Voices buzzed through her blue-tooth earpiece and echoed in her head. Candace was explaining why the wrong art had been sent to big-ass-client Number One, how prototype designs had been shown to a group they weren't meant for, and that it came down to Tori not reminding Candace to do her job.

"This is Mary." A smooth voice came over the line.

Tori bit back the retort that they all knew who she was. The Vice President of Client Relations didn't let anyone forget who she was.

"Tell me, Victoria," Mary continued. "You knew this was a critical step and what kind of deadlines we were under. Why didn't you check the art before it went to the client?"

Because that was what she paid Candace to do. Tori choked on the snide response. "I didn't think I would need to—"

"What didn't you understand about *mission critical*?"

Tori gave up keeping track of who was saying what. She knew all of the people by voice, but at this point, they were slinging shit at her. She muted her phone as another conversation erupted about why this happened, and she collapsed on her couch. Why couldn't she defend herself? That was the root of everything. She couldn't stand up for herself at work. She couldn't tell Archer why she was really upset.

Someone knocked on the front door, and she hesitated. She tuned back into the phone conversation long enough to realize they weren't going to ask for her input, and even if they did, they wouldn't listen, so she decided to answer.

Unexpected tears stung her eyelids when she saw the large teddy bear holding a bouquet of daises and roses. The delivery guy handed over the bundle. "Victoria Goode?"

She nodded and took the stuffed animal from him. He flashed her a wooden smile, already turning away as he said, "Have a nice day."

She extracted the flowers and set them on an end table, until she could dig up a vase. Her heart hammered a million miles a minute, as she pulled out the white envelope peeking up from the top. A typed script font read, *If you won't let me be there for you, maybe you'll let this take my place. Archer.*

A few tears escaped and trickled down her cheek, and she sniffled them back. She grabbed the bear by the hand, thoughts a jumble, and dragged it back with her. The stuffed animal was huge; it had to be at least three feet. She sat it next to her on the couch and then turned back to her laptop, though nothing was happening there, since everyone was on the phone call.

Then she realized something didn't sound right. The buzzing in her ear had gone silent.

"Victoria," Mary said, "are you still there? Do you have us on mute?"

Shit. Tori unmuted the phone. "I'm sorry. I'm still here."

"Dana asked what you have to say for yourself."

The haughty question snapped something inside. How dare Archer think he could apologize with a bunch of gorgeous flowers? Why the hell did her employees think they could push this on her? Who the fuck were these people, to think they could walk all over her?

"I'll tell you what I have to say for myself." Tori's words were cold and removed even to her own ears, and she sank into the verbal ice, letting it encase and drive her. "I'm not the lackey you bitch at, because someone pissed in your coffee this morning. I'm fucking co-owner of this business, and you people work for me. And somehow this mess is my fault because I didn't... what? Do your jobs for you? Because I didn't anticipate you people were incompetent?"

Her messenger on her laptop chimed, and she ignored it. She was going to speak her mind. "Every time something happens, not only am I on call—even if it's two on a Sunday morning—but I spend the next twelve hours telling each and every one of you, individually, why it happened, trying to be politically correct and not cast blame. I spend more of my life reassuring you I have things under control, than I do actually controlling them."

Her messenger chimed, again.

"I'm sick of you not doing what you were hired for. Of you taking advantage of the fact I'm a lax manager. And maybe you ought to take a look at your operations as a whole, before you continue to lay blame on a single individual—"

"Did I miss something?" Brad cut over the line.

Great. Someone tattled to her brother. How *fourth grade* of them. "Not at all. I've got this under control," she said.

"Fantastic." A strain bled into Brad's words. Would anyone but her hear that? "And I know this is urgent, ladies and gentlemen, but Tori and I have a family emergency, and I need her help. You can all take care of yourselves for a moment, right?"

She swallowed a growl and tried to sound as professional as he did. "I'll speak with you, folks, later." She disconnected and threw the phone aside.

A series of notes from Brad sat waiting on her messenger.

Mary emailed me. What's going on?

Tori, this isn't the way to handle this.

You're frustrated. I get it. Take this offline with me, so we can figure out a solution.

Now, please.

She sent him back a note.

Fine. I'm done. You've been telling me for years to take a stand, and now I'm not doing it right? What do you want from me?

She flopped back on the couch, confusion, anger, frustration, and betrayal battling for her attention. She didn't know how much time had passed—ten minutes or half an hour—when her phone rang.

"Hello." Her voice was flat.

"What the hell was that?" Brad's voice was loud enough to rattle her brain.

She turned down the volume on her phone. Fresh tears pricked her eyelids. Damn it. What was wrong with her? She couldn't lose it now. But she couldn't find the right words.

When she didn't answer, he continued—hell, he might've continued anyway. "We had members of senior management from every branch of the company on that call. I'm glad you're doing something about Candace, but this isn't how you handle disputes."

She managed to find her voice. "It's how *they* handle disputes. You missed the ninety minutes of them dragging me through the mud."

"If you want to flog one or more of those people privately—or even publicly—and they deserve it, that's fine. You've got the authority to do that, and you never exercise it. But you can't tear into them without focus. If you want them to take you seriously, this isn't the way to do it."

"Fire me." She expected the words to taste bitter, but they were the best part of the conversation.

"Not funny. Candace has already filed a complaint with HR. Says you're harassing her. I *know* you're not. I've got your back on this. You're not wrong, and I'm not upset at you. I'm a lot concerned that you snapped. What do you need from me, to get through this?"

A different job. A new perspective. She didn't know. "I'm fine."

"Tori—"

"I'll be okay. I promise." It took a force of will she didn't think she had, to keep her tone steady. Would he buy it? "It's been a bad day, but I've got it now."

"All right. But call me if you need me."

"Sure. Always." She dropped her phone, and the impact of the conference call and Brad's follow-up slammed into her. She wanted to be furious with him for stopping her, but she couldn't find fault in his words. She tore out her earpiece and flung it across the room. The rubber and plastic bounced off the far wall and clattered to the floor with an unsatisfactory *plink*.

She couldn't hold back the tears anymore. Fuck. How could she get out of this? She grabbed the teddy bear, squeezed it to her chest, and rolled to her side, unable to stop the sobs that racked through her.

chapter thirteen

Archer glared at the analytics for his website. Given some time and a lot more work, he could probably make the site take off. Online sales were up this month, and at this pace, it could be the thing that saved the shop.

Right. And if he willed the numbers to change, three extra zeroes might appear at the end. It sounded as effective as anything else he'd tried.

He sat in his office—a tiny room tucked behind the main store, which had been a walk-in pantry at earlier points in its life—hoping he'd find a new answer if he stared at figures long enough. He wasn't picky where the numbers came from. At this point, he was tempted to write down a few random ones, to have something positive to look at.

He pushed aside his laptop and flopped back in his office chair. If he was willing to tighten his belt, cut his salary, make sure the middle-floor apartments were never empty—and raise the rent fifty bucks a month—and stop hosting the anime club, or at least stop paying to feed them, he could make things work.

Maybe he could call Gwen or Zane and ask for

some help with the search-engine keywords. As soon as the thought formed, he knew it was a bad one. Without Tori, he didn't have any connection to Gwen, and he was lucky Zane hadn't brained him for what he'd pulled with Riley. What the hell had he been thinking? Why did being around Riley do that to him?

The train of thought was derailed by memories of Tori's reaction, and the fact she still wasn't speaking to him. Well, that wasn't completely true. She had texted him a *thank you* for the flowers. He sighed. Forget about Zane or Riley. How was he going to make things better with Tori?

He probably wasn't. He turned his attention back to the website. He was on his own for all of this.

Derrek knocked on the door frame at the same time he poked his head around the corner. "Elliot's here."

"Send him back." Something told Archer he didn't want to be having this conversation, but there was no reason to be rude.

A moment later, Elliot dropped into the padded chair across from Archer's desk and kicked his feet onto a nearby banker's box. He set his briefcase on the floor next to him. "How's business?"

"Same old stuff. Still feeding people's addictions."

"We've finalized the details on our sponsorship program." Elliot grabbed something from the side pocket of his case and slid it across the desk.

This again? Archer kept his pleasant smile in place. "That's nice."

"This is a preliminary contract. You can have a

lawyer look it over, and all that stuff. The terms are pretty straightforward. We pay you a fixed amount every month—basically an advertising fee—and you agree to feature our comics in your storefront. You don't have to carry us exclusively, and there aren't currently any restrictions on how many of their books you stock versus ours. As long as you make sure we get top billing."

Archer nodded, to indicate he understood. Such a bad idea. He liked Elliot well enough—the only rep he had, who stopped by regularly and was friendly—but Elliot's company wasn't his top seller, and they didn't provide him with any merchandise to back up the comic sales. Archer would be sacrificing prime real estate, to sign this deal.

"You're not considering it. Are you?" Elliot grabbed the contract off the desk.

"Nope."

"Did you hear Tori out?"

"You talked to Tori about this?"

Elliot shrugged. "I'm surprised she didn't say something. Well, no. Actually, I'm not."

Archer wasn't either, but he didn't like the disdain in the other man's voice. "Don't drag her into this. And what the hell kind of ethics are you practicing, to go behind my back and discuss my business with someone else?"

"But it's not just about you." Elliot folded back the pages of the contract and placed it in front of Archer again. "Addendum A says she gets a cut and your cut grows, if she's willing to make one costume a week, to our specifications, for display in your store."

A foreign kind of frustration and impotence poured through Archer. On one hand, not only did he need another revenue stream, but this could give Tori the encouragement she needed to do more with her talent. On the other, something didn't feel right about the deal. That didn't mean he liked her keeping the information from him. "What Tori does is her decision."

"Really? What makes you think she'd seize something like this without someone pushing her every step of the way?"

"Excuse me?"

"I'm giving both of you an excellent chance. You know—*know*—that left to her own devices, she'll let this opportunity rot. She doesn't have the confidence, she doesn't have the balls, and she'd rather someone else took the reins and gave her a direction."

"Get out." Archer was on his feet before he could process what he was doing.

"I'm sorry?"

"You're not." Archer clenched his hands by his sides. "I won't listen to you talk about anyone like that, especially not her."

"The truth hurts."

"Get the *fuck* out."

"Call me when you see the light." Elliot nodded at the contract, never flinching. "The offer won't be good for long."

Archer held back his roar, but only barely. He dropped back into his chair, hands still shaking. He didn't know which of Elliot's assumptions bothered him the most. The one thing he knew was he owed

Tori a serious apology.

Besides, he wanted to see her. Needed to talk to her. Was desperate to hold her. He paused as the desires sank in and took root. It was as if every thought of Tori had crawled under his skin.

It should bother him. Getting involved so deeply with someone, relying so heavily on having them around, was what had gotten him in trouble in his last relationship.

Except this was different. Riley was an impulse, but Tori was an addictive, wonderful, all-consuming need. And he wanted to feed that craving.

He grabbed his keys and cut a straight line for the front door. "I'll be back later," he called to Derrek as the door swung shut behind him. "Close up if I'm not."

"Got it." Derrek's response was muffled by the glass, as the door swung shut.

Archer was grateful Tori lived close, but the drive still seemed to take forever. He pulled into the visitor parking next to her condo, shut off the engine, and sprinted up the steps to her place.

Please let her answer. He couldn't help his smile when her door swung open.

She didn't look quite as happy to see him. "Hey." She stepped aside and gestured for him to come in.

He stopped immediately inside, unable to wait any longer, to say what he was thinking. "I'm sorry," he blurted out. "About what happened with Riley the other day; about brushing you aside because she was around; about whatever else I may have done to hurt you…"

The corners of her mouth tugged up, but her eyes still looked sad. "It's all right." She nodded to the couch. "Do you want to stick around for a little bit?"

"What's going on?" He hated her sorrow, but he had no idea how to erase it. Something thrummed in his chest when he saw the large teddy bear sitting in one of the easy chairs. He dropped on the couch and patted the cushion next to him.

"Work shit. Same old stuff," she said.

Right. That. One of those things he couldn't threaten for her or make go away, regardless of how much he wanted to. "Want to talk about it?"

"No." She straddled his legs and draped her arms around his neck. "Talking doesn't solve as many things as you think."

He hadn't expected this. Almost a week of not speaking to him, and now she sat in his lap. Every time she shifted her weight, she rubbed his cock through his jeans. He hardened under the attention.

He needed to find out where the sudden one-eighty came from. He dug his fingers into her hips, and he exhaled through clenched teeth. This felt incredible. He wanted to let her drive the moment as much as he wanted to know what was going on. It wouldn't solve anything, but they could work that out later, right?

He didn't resist when she pressed her lips to his, hungry and desperate. Fuck. She tasted amazing. She trailed her nails along the back of his neck, and he ran his fingers up her spine to clasp her head and hold her in place. She whimpered and ground against him.

Something salty mingled with the kiss, and his gut sank. He broke away, his heart crashing at the sight of her tears.

chapter fourteen

When Archer showed up, Tori was seconds away from telling him to go to hell. But the confrontation with her employees left her drained, and she wanted Archer. His comfort. And desperately to not think.

For a moment after she climbed in his lap, she thought he was going to tell her *no*. Then his body responded, and he did as well. It wasn't a solution, but she wanted to not feel the emotional pain. To only experience the bliss of his touch. When she kissed him, he grabbed back, and she threw herself into the physical. She could cope with the rest later. This would be a salve on her wounds.

Except the tears sliding down her face betrayed her, and she couldn't hold them back. He broke the kiss, searching her gaze with concern.

"Shit. Tori, no." He moved his hand to her cheek and brushed away the tears.

She shook her head and tried to lean in for another kiss.

He placed a palm on her chest, keeping the distance between them. "Talk to me, please?"

"No." She snarled and tore away, clambering to

her feet. "I don't want to talk about this, because our relationship is about sex. Not baring our souls."

"Except we had friendship first. The sex isn't worth it if we lose that."

The words cut deep, drawing out more tears. She ran the back of her hand across her cheeks. "Damn it, Archer. You can't have it both ways. It's supposed to be *no strings*. That's why it's okay for you to throw yourself at your ex-girlfriend in front of me?" She choked on the words, but she couldn't stop. "Or maybe that doesn't matter, since it doesn't seem to bother you she's taken."

"I shouldn't have acted the way I did with Riley. But this won't fix it."

"*Nothing* can fix this." It took the last of her restraint to not scream. "There are no easy solutions for us. For work. For life. I don't think there are any solutions at all."

"There's an answer. There's always an answer."

"Stop." Desperation filled her "I don't want this. I don't want you to be reasonable and rational. I want you to fuck my brains out, so I don't have to think about what's going on for a few minutes."

"Has it worked so far?"

"Temporarily."

"Is it what you really want?"

"Yes." Her voice cracked, and she swallowed to try and clear out the raw ache in her throat. "Or are you going to tell me you know better, the way you always do with Riley?"

"No." He rested his hand on the back of her neck, palm brushing her cheekbone. "I'm here for you. I'll do what you want, because honestly, I don't have enough strength to tell you *no* another time."

She pressed against him, fisted her fingers in his hair, and yanked his mouth to hers. She poured all her frustration, her need, and her every last exposed nerve into the kiss. He growled and drew her closer, pressing his frame against her.

She felt wetness on her cheeks, and she broke away with a sob she couldn't stop. She wrapped her arms around herself, trying to keep her body from shaking, but it didn't work.

"Fuck." A larger, stronger pair of arms circled her, and Archer drew her in.

She buried her head against his chest, unable to control the wails wrenching from deep inside. She didn't know what she was going to do. About him. About work. About any of it. God damn it—when did life get so complicated? And why couldn't she stop crying?

He moved his lips against the top of her head, murmuring sounds that didn't mean anything, but soothed her anyway. As her sobs slowed, he led her back to the couch. He dropped ono the center cushion and tugged her in his lap.

She curled up, listening to his heart and letting the steady rhythm calm her. Neither of them spoke for a while, even after she brought her outburst under control.

"I'll only ask one more time, I promise. Do you want to talk about it?" he asked

She did. So very much. She wanted to spill her guts and tell him how much work sucked and how much she wished she'd never let Brad talk her into taking that stupid job, and how much she was falling for Archer. She winced mentally as soon as the last thought crossed her mind. This was bad. She couldn't do this. Archer was off limits. He would break her heart, because regardless of his apology, he still had issues with Riley.

She managed to say, "I do, but not tonight."

"I'm here when you're ready." He trailed his fingers through her hair and pressed his lips to her forehead.

She pushed closer, wanting to lose herself in him. If she couldn't have him for good, she was going to enjoy him while he was here. "You don't have to go home, do you?"

"I don't have to be anywhere but here."

♥ ♥ ♥

Tori snuggled into the strong body behind her, pulling Archer's arm tighter. She'd slept better last night than in ages. They watched the worst movies, and somewhere around midnight or one, they'd lost their jeans and climbed into bed. As far as she remembered, she fell asleep the moment he wrapped himself around her.

Too bad she had to face reality. She forced her eyes open and scowled when she saw what time it was. "Damn it," she muttered.

"How do you have a *damn it* before eight in the morning?" He rested his chin on her shoulder.

She smiled and leaned her cheek against his. Now her head was clearer, life didn't seem quite as bleak, but she wasn't looking forward to what came next. "I have a conference call with Candace and HR in thirty minutes.”

“Do you have breakfast ingredients in the house?” He trailed his fingers lightly along her hip, up the elastic of her panties, and back down her hip.

“Probably. I can make oatmeal.”

“Get ready for your call. I’ll make food.”

She couldn’t let him do that; it was too tempting, too comfortable, too much something she wanted to get used to. Still, she couldn’t force herself to turn him down. “If you’re sure.”

“Positive.”

Disappointment trickled in as cool air met her now-exposed back, but it was tempered when he grabbed her hand and pulled her into a sitting position. “Get dressed, bring your phone into the kitchen for your call, and I’ll take care of the rest.”

“All right.” She had to bite her tongue, to keep from asking if he wanted to join her in the shower. There was no way she was embarrassing herself like she had last night. Besides, she didn’t have enough time.

She showered quickly, dressed, and ran a brush through her hair, before pulling it back in a ponytail. The familiar smells of Archer’s cooking greeted her, as she stepped into the living room, and she closed her eyes.

He slid a plate across the table. Pancakes. Except, she didn’t have any pancake mix in the house. He’d made it from scratch?

And then she saw the time, and her enjoyment scurried to someplace unknown, replaced with a sick clawing in the bottom of her stomach.

“I’m sorry.” She slipped in her ear piece and

waited for the phone to ring. She really didn't want to take this call.

"Do what you have to. I'll stick around until you're done."

She picked at her food, torn between enjoying it and the growing uneasiness in her gut. She dialed into the conference number, and the robotic voice told her she was the second person on the line. She and Michelle from HR made small talk for a few moments. How were Michelle's kids? Was Tori looking forward to the company picnic this weekend?

Damn. Tori forgot about that, and she'd never hear the end of it from Brad if she skipped out.

The clock hit eight thirty and then rolled past it. It figured; Candace was late.

Tori jumped when the line chimed a few minutes later, indicating a third party had joined the call. She shot Archer another look, and he smiled in return. She steeled herself and answered the phone.

"Hi, Candace. This is Michelle in HR."

"Hi, Michelle."

Tori swallowed again. She could do this.

"I have Tori on the line with us today. Do you mind if I explain what this call is about, to make sure we're all on the same page?"

Maybe this wouldn't be too bad. Michelle was a great arbitrator. This call was her idea, when Tori talked to her about Candace's complaint. A way to get both sides of the story, and ultimately decide how to handle Candace, in a neutral forum.

"That's fine." Candace's tone was snipped.

"I read your complaint that you feel harassed,

and I take that seriously. From a management perspective, Tori explained to me there are certain issues with some of your work and behavior," Michelle said. "This call is a chance for you to explain to me your side of the story, so I can make sure everyone is treated fairly. Does that make sense?"

Tori liked this letting-Michelle-do-the-talking thing.

"Yes," Candace said.

"So in your own words, explain to me why you belittled a member of executive management, in front of the entire senior staff."

Tori's confidence in the smooth nature of the call fled. That didn't sound like a nonjudgmental question. Brad had interfered.

"That wasn't my intention." Candace sounded as calm and removed as always. "I was frustrated, because I didn't feel Tori was hearing what I had to say."

"Mhmm." Michelle paused. "I apologize if there are stretches of silence. I want to write this all down, to make sure I get it accurate."

Archer caught her attention, his brows knitted together, corners of his mouth tugged down.

She tried to give him a smile, but it felt more like a grimace, upon delivery. His frown grew, and she turned away so she could focus on the call.

"Have you tried to express these concerns in the past?" Michelle spoke again.

"Of course. Ms. Goode doesn't like to hear those things that make her less than happy."

Fury sped into Tori's veins. "That's not entirely

accurate. In fact, it's not even close to correct."

"Tori, we need to let Candace talk now."

The conversation deteriorated from there, as Candace used each question to redirect the blame to Tori again and again, for her inability to discipline her employee. By the time Michelle was done with her questions, Tori bit the inside of her cheek, to keep from repeating her performance on the other day's call.

"Thank you for your time, Candace." Michelle's polite tone cut like a cheese grater now. "Tori and I need to discuss the next steps to take, and she'll be in touch with you by the end of next week, at the latest."

"Next week?" Candace's question was laced with disdain.

"Yes. We have a number of factors to consider." Tori couldn't keep the edge from her voice. She wanted to fire Candace right now, but there were legal factors to consider.

"Just know, if you lay me off, I will haunt you. I will sue you from every angle possible, for wrongful termination and discrimination. I'll drag your company through the muck so far, you won't recognize your own public image when you're done." Candace clicked off the line before Tori could reply.

Tori stared blankly at her phone. "Can she do that?" she asked Michelle. Speaking her mind was supposed to make life easier, not give her more hoops to jump through. "Can I fire her now, for threatening me?" Who the fuck wanted to work for a company they despised as much as Candace seemed to hate theirs?

"She can try. Anyone can file a lawsuit. That's why we have to make absolute certain we go about this the right way."

"I understand. I want her gone, though. Am I allowed to say that?"

"Yeah." Michelle sighed. "I'll get you the paperwork. Dot every *I*, cross every *T*, and have Legal sign off on it when you're done."

They exchanged a few more pleasantries before disconnecting, but Tori's mind had already leaped ahead to the dread of having to lay someone off.

"That didn't sound like sunshine and rainbows." Archer nudged her plate toward her, concern heavy on his face.

"It could've been worse. It could've been a lot better, but hey, I'll probably fire the biggest pain in my ass ever. Yay?"

"Um… I guess?"

She didn't want to talk about Candace, but the call had reminded her of something else. She took a bite of the food, trying to focus on the way it tasted, instead of the sickness churning in her gut. "I need a favor." The moment the words crossed her lips, she cringed. Riley's voice echoed in her skull, saying the same thing.

His expression faltered but then returned to reassuring. "Name it."

"Our company picnic is this weekend. I don't suppose you'll be my backup?" She didn't deserve to ask him, but she couldn't walk into that crowd alone, when it was smattered with unfriendly faces. Candace still worked for them, and Mary would be there. Not everyone in the company hated Tori, but the anticipation of a few was enough to set her on edge.

"Absolutely," Arched said.

She could do this. Archer was charming, so the other executives would love him, and she hated speaking her mind anyway, so it shouldn't be a problem to keep her mouth shut. The picnic wouldn't be a big deal. Would it?

chapter fifteen

Archer had to navigate several rows of cars at the edge of the park, before he found an empty spot. Each time he turned a corner, Tori's grip on his leg tightened. He finally negotiated them into an opening and shut off the engine. He pried her hand away from his knee and intertwined his fingers with hers, giving her a gentle squeeze. "This'll be fine."

She exhaled loudly. "I know."

The moment they were out of the car and standing side by side, she slipped her hand into his again. It hadn't taken much prodding for her to tell him exactly how much she dreaded this afternoon. She was apologetic and gave him several opportunities to back out, but he was happy to stand by her side.

Part of him knew it might become a problem if he figured out which of these assholes made Tori's life so miserable, but he kept that bit on a leash. He didn't want to make things worse for her.

She pulled him toward the large crowd under one of the pavilions, her company's logo glaring back at them from the banner waving in the breeze. The tame and family-friendly party was an odd sight, since this group made money selling sexy underwear. Laughter mingled with chatter, as adults grouped together. Children rushed around their legs and tumbled on the grass and playground.

"*Tori.*" A loud squeal cut above it all, and seconds later, a dark haired girl attached herself to Tori in a huge hug.

Tori ruffled the girl's curls. "Hey, Drea."

Archer had heard Tori's niece's name before, but never met the girl. She looked a lot like her father.

Drea turned her attention to Archer, blue eyes narrow as she looked him up and down. "Is this your boyfriend?"

Boyfriend. Archer liked the sound of that. The realization hit him hard, and he gripped it tight.

Tori's cheeks turned several shades redder. "Well, he's a boy, and he is a friend."

He couldn't ignore the sting of the awkward brush off.

"What's your name?" Drea continued to scrutinize him.

"Archer."

She seemed to consider this for a moment, and then broke out in a sing-song voice. "Tori and Archer sittin' in a tree. K-I-S-S-I-N-G. First—"

"I'll get you." Tori tickled the younger girl.

Drea squealed and backed away. "You can't do that. I'll karate chop you." She lunged forward, hand extended, and brought the edge of her palm down on Tori's shoulder.

Tori grunted and rolled onto her back, holding her neck. "Oh, you got me."

Drea giggled and knelt in front of her. "You're

such a child."

Tori stuck out her tongue. "I'm not a child; you're a child."

Archer watched the exchange, a mixture of fascination and adoration flowing through him. He'd seen Tori with the younger customers in the comic store, so he knew she was good with kids, but this was different. She completely lost herself in the moment. It was beautiful.

"Tori." A familiar voice cut a jagged path through the fun.

Tori and Drea were on their feet in a second. Tori smiled at Brad, but Archer could tell it was an almost painful gesture for her.

Tori pulled a five from her wallet and handed it to Drea. "Ask your dad if you can get your face painted."

"Daddy?"

"Of course, sweetie." Brad patted her on the shoulder and pointed her toward a table with a line of children leading to it. "Stay where I can see you."

Tori took a step back. "Big turn out."

Archer'd never heard her use that tone with Brad before. Not that he watched the two of them together a lot, but they tended to get along. Made business run easier, and all that. Archer rested a hand at the small of her back. Her spine was rigid, but she leaned into the contact.

Brad's smile was big enough to show off teeth, but his eyes were flat. "Morgan is minding the grill. He was asking about you."

"I'll have to find him and say *hello*."

Archer resisted the urge to squirm, as the tension

built. It gnawed at him to not be able to do anything but stand there.

Brad stepped closer, and his voice dropped in volume. "Michelle told me how things went with Candace. Are you holding together?"

If Tori's smile had been strained before, it was nothing compared to the stretched-tight look she wore now. "I'm sure I'm fine. You didn't have to check up on me."

"Candace threatened to sue *us*. You and me? You know, the people who own the company? I'd rather have heard it from you."

Archer ground his teeth together.

"I've got it under control," Tori said.

"That's great. I'd still like to be kept in the loop," Brad said.

Archer wanted to be anywhere but here. This was too private a conversation, for him to be party to. He opened his mouth, to excuse himself, but a freight train of words cut him off.

"What do you want from me?" An edge lined Tori's words. "One day you're telling me I need to learn to handle things on my own, and now you want every detail of every minute of my working day?"

Nearby heads turned in their direction. Archer slid his hand to Tori's hip and squeezed lightly.

Brad narrowed his eyes. "That's not what I'm say—"

"Stop." Tori never raised her voice, but there was a force behind it Archer had never heard before. "I'm so sick of this. I'm not saying I've never made a mistake, but *holy fuck*. I told you I didn't want this job. I insisted I wasn't cut out for it, and you all but bulldozed me into it."

"You always could have said *no*."

"I am now." She clenched her hands into fists. A low murmur spread through the group of onlookers, and all gazes in the crowd were trained on them. She either didn't notice or didn't care. "No. No. No."

This was going beyond standing up for herself. Archer was torn between letting her speak and prompting her to stop. She was going to regret the attention and the fight with Brad, once her anger ebbed, but Archer was also relieved and a little pleased she took a stand.

Tori stood nose to nose with Brad now. An impressive feat, given he was almost a foot taller. "I'm going to leave. Go ahead and say whatever you'd like, once I'm gone. Just know I don't want to hear it. Leave me out of your plans. If you don't think I can do this, stop expecting me to."

She reached behind her and intertwined her fingers with Archer's, as she stepped away from a narrow-eyed Brad. "Can we go now?" Her voice was barely a squeak, only meant for Archer's ears.

He nodded and steered her to the parking lot. Her gait was stiff, her grip tight.

She didn't say another word as they made their way to the car. She was silent as Archer held the door for her, and he watched her drop into the passenger seat. Her jaw stayed clenched, and her gaze fixed straight ahead, as he pulled onto the main road.

He should say something. Tell her she was right to do what she had or that it would be okay or something reassuring. But he didn't know if she would believe him. Hell, he didn't know if he believed it. He pulled into the lane to turn right toward her condo.

"I don't want to go home." She shattered the silence.

He couldn't argue with that. He had zero desire to deny her anything. "Do you want to hang with me?"

"Please. But no people."

"All right." Fifteen minutes later, he parked the car in its spot back home and helped her out. He'd already told Derrek he'd be out for the afternoon, so he avoided the store and headed straight for the back entrance.

She gripped his hand as they climbed the stairs to his apartment. Inside, he pointed her toward the couch, pulled up the most mindless, funny movie he could think of to stream, and then took the spot next to her. The moment he sat, she scooted close. Legs tucked to the side, she rested her head on his shoulder. He wrapped an arm around her. The posture felt natural and right. Comforting. He only hoped it was—at least a little—the same for her, because he had no idea how to reassure her otherwise, and her blank-eyed-stare drove a spike through him.

They'd figure it out. Or she'd figure it out, and he'd support whatever she decided. Unless her solution was to apologize on Monday, swear never to do it again, and go back to the way things had been. He didn't know if he could support that.

Minutes ticked away, and the movie whirred on, but he didn't pay attention. His focus was on the warm body curled against him. Had she fallen asleep?

"I'm tired of running away." Her comment startled him.

He muted the TV in an instant, not wanting to miss a single quiet word. He also didn't want to say anything that might stop her talking. "Okay."

"I've never told anyone the real reason I moved here." She trailed a finger down his chest, and a pleasant chill ran through him. He needed to focus on what she said, not what she did.

"To finish college?"

He felt, more than heard, her laugh. She flattened her hand against his chest, the heat of her palm seeping through his shirt and warming his skin. "No," she said. "I mean it was a side effect, but no. My freshman year of college, I was like any other noob. Lost, terrified, and looking for someone I could relate to. That someone was Nick, and even though we'd only been dating a few weeks when he told me he loved me, I figured he must have it right, so I said the same in return."

"Okay?" It took focus for him not to tense at the story. His insides clenched at the thought of Tori professing her love for anyone. It wasn't a rational reaction, but he didn't care.

"We moved in together before first year was up. Life wasn't the mad, passionate fling movies say it should be, and he certainly wasn't the bumbling goofball anime led me to believe most boys were, but I knew it was real life. School and work were stressful, so it was okay if we rarely saw each other. He almost always stayed up until after I was gone for the day, so we rarely slept together. He tended to shrug off my advances most the time, but we were in love, right?"

He wouldn't clench his fists. He wouldn't stiffen up. He was going to listen patiently to her story.

She patted his chest. "Breathe."

He forced himself to exhale.

"It's okay; this is the past now." Her light laugh broke some of the tension, but it didn't erase it completely.

"If you're all right, I am."

"I'm still working on *all right*." She pressed closer, resting a warm cheek against him. "We talked about marriage, because that's what people in love do, and we agreed we'd wait until after we both graduated. It wasn't formal, just this vague kind of goal for the future. And then, one night he didn't come home."

She went rigid against him. It took a few minutes before she continued. "I was panicked, and I called the police, and they told me it hadn't been long enough to consider him a missing person, but they'd take my information and I could call again if he was still missing the next day. As soon as I gave them his name and a description, the dispatcher started laughing."

"What?" Archer hadn't expected that. Out of all the possible scenarios that usually went with this kind of story, it wasn't one that had crossed his mind.

"They already knew where he was, because they had him in a holding cell. Indecent exposure charges."

Had the guy been a pervert? Worse?

"Apparently, he got drunk the night before and

decided three in the morning was the perfect time to show up on his girl's porch and propose."

"Did you sleep through it or something?" he asked.

"No. The dispatcher was laughing because Nick had picked the wrong porch. And was naked. Ha-ha. It was drunken foolishness—wasn't that cute? Stupid but adorable. The entire station was talking about it. That's what she said to me. When she gave me the address he visited instead, I knew it hadn't been a mistake. It was where his ex-girlfriend lived. His high-school sweetheart. The woman he still kept pictures of in his desk drawer that I pretended weren't a big deal. The house he would go out of his way to drive by, always telling me he wanted to take the long way home.

"And best of all"—the joy was gone from her punctuated laughs—"she was the one who bailed him out. I didn't need to pick him up, because the nice lady he harassed had already taken care of everything."

His fingers ached, and he unclenched them from the cushion he'd been gripping. He flexed a few times, to work the kinks from his knuckles. "I'm sorry."

"I was, too. I couldn't face him; I was so embarrassed. I packed everything, left him a note that said *goodbye*, drained my bank account, and got in the car and drove to another state, because Brad said I could crash with him for a while. I wondered for months after if I overreacted. Until my mother sent me a newspaper clipping—their wedding announcement."

Archer had no idea how to respond. No wonder

she was edgy about Riley. He had a feeling there was something, but nothing could have prepared him for this.

"And I still wish I'd told him off. It eats at me that I never said anything to his face. I'm tired of holding it all back, but I don't like the consequences either. God. The things I said to Brad today… He's always been there for me. Amazing older brother, and all that. He was by my side through that break-up. And I threw a tantrum today, in front of our fucking company, when he was completely right."

"He's not *completely* right. And talking it out with him *will* help." Archer rested his hand over hers and traced his thumb over her knuckles. "It's not always easy, but it eliminates a lot of regrets and what-if's."

"Is that why you act the way you do around Riley? Regret?" Her voice was low, but he heard every word as if she'd shouted.

He opened his mouth, but no response came out. He couldn't find the words to explain. But he needed to.

She cut him off. "Forget it. I didn't ask. Tonight, I don't want to know."

He needed to tell her. It had nothing to do with lingering feelings, and everything to do with making sure he didn't make the same mistake with the right woman. With Tori.

The revelation hit him hard. She really was that one person. Thinking he might have to give up her company—or worse, that he might be the reason she felt unhappy—was enough to crunch his chest into a tight ball. He had to answer her question. He had to let her know there were no regrets about his past. That the only thing he'd regret would be screwing things up with her. "It's—"

"It's okay." The sadness in her voice belied the reassurance. "Or it will be, one way or another."

His heart gnawed at his ribs, frustration and concern warring for attention. How was he going to make this better?

chapter sixteen

Tori tried not to count her steps, as she strode toward the *Too Goode* corporate offices. The weekend at Archer's had been tense at first, but things calmed down on Sunday. She didn't make it home until this morning, and she was only there long enough to get ready for her meeting with Brad. When she asked for his time, he agreed without hesitation. The cloud that lingered after she'd spilled her guts about her ex to Archer, was nothing compared to the dread enveloping her now.

She forced her feet forward, one in front of the other, toward the office at the end of the hall. The door was open, but Brad's attention was on his computer.

He didn't look up when he nodded to the chair across from him. "Have a seat. I'll be with you shortly."

She meant it when she said she was tired of running away. Regardless of how much she needed to set things straight with Brad, she wasn't going to roll over and play dead, either. She had every intention of being polite, but she was also going to be heard.

"I'm sorry about that." Brad finally turned to her. "I'm glad you reached out to me."

"Of course."

He leaned forward, hands clasped. "I know we're both busy, so I apologize if I seem abrupt, but I'd like to cut to why we're here."

The cold tone in his voice and the stone mask, meant to draw the other person out and let them expose their thoughts before he showed his hand, gnawed at her. This was the same thing Gwen did with her nephews, in Archer's shop, and she learned it from Brad. "Don't do this to me." Tori tried to ignore the churning nerves in her gut. The rush of knowing she was going to do this was incredible but nauseating. "Don't turn this kind of manipulation on me."

"If I'm more direct, will you answer my question this time, instead of insisting you're fine? What's going on with you?"

Tori spent the morning rehearsing in her head every direction this conversation could go as well as her possible responses. The moment he asked the direct question, any answer she had vanished.

Her mind whirred for a response, while Brad continued. "I don't want to do this with you, Tori. We're supposed to put on a united front, not bicker like children."

You don't like it? Fire me. The same thought as Saturday. And the moment it crossed her mind, an odd calm coursed through her veins. "Maybe we can't do it. You're good at this. I'm not. It's time to stop pretending."

"That's not what I'm saying." Brad scrubbed

his face and let out a long sigh. "If you were having problems, why didn't you come to me?"

This was her chance to make things right, though. He was offering an olive branch. "I didn't think I could."

"You *always* can."

"That's not what I meant." Damn it. She swallowed and searched for something stronger. Something to make herself understood. "The conversation never changes. I tell you I'm not comfortable with confrontation and discipline, and you tell me I'll learn."

"I'm sorry. I don't understand—"

"And that's the problem." Something inside Tori snapped, as if the tight line running through her had broken and slapped her with the recoil. "You can't see this from my perspective. I want to be creating. I thought that's what I'd be doing when we set this up."

"You are. And we can get you more of that. You don't want to manage anymore? Fine. We'll move those people under someone else. Mary, maybe. She's anxious to talk to both of us right now. This'll make her happy."

"But I'm not creating. Not free-form. This isn't me saying, *ooh, pretty, let's do that*. It's some corporate asshole in Phoenix saying, *I saw this on Adult Swim. It's popular now, right?*" Tori smiled, but she didn't feel any joy.

"Corporate asshole like me?"

"That's not what I meant." She was saying that a lot. Why was he twisting her words? Or maybe she was doing that poor a job of expressing herself.

Brad drummed his fingers on the desk, as if collecting his thoughts. "I want to find a happy middle ground here, but this is a business. We have to make what people are buying, or we don't sell. It's also *our* business. I can't do it without you."

"I don't know what to tell you." She saw his point, but it didn't change the way she felt about the situation. That her dissatisfaction with the entire arrangement had grown over the past few years, festering.

"Figure it out. Tell me what it is you want. Not what I think is best or this vague notion of *I'm not happy* or what you assume I want to hear, and we'll make it happen."

The offer rolled around in her thoughts, nudging all her complaints. Bouncing off frustration. Collecting everything that had built inside.

"I heard you met Gwen's nephews the other day." Brad's out-of-the-blue comment knocked Tori off kilter.

The memory of that day in the comic shop added to the churning inside. "That's one way to put it."

"She and her brother have a really shitty relationship. Worse, since she had his kids sent to Juvie. Watching them for the day was kind of her last attempt to reconcile with him, but he's not interested in that."

"I didn't have any idea."

"Because she doesn't talk about it. They were best friends growing up, and it kills her that they're not anymore. They lost their chance."

A dim light clicked on in Tori's skull. "We

haven't. Have we?"

"God, I hope not. We had a fight at a company picnic. We'll make it better. But I don't have any desire for that to be us. Tell me what's going to make you happy."

"I can't." Her choices warred inside. Quit. Walk away from this and go do her own thing, and leave Brad stranded. Or stay on and stay miserable.

"You keep asking me to fire you. Is that what you really want?"

Why was he forcing this on her? "Yes. No. I don't know. Maybe."

His frown made the gears in her head spin faster. Work harder for a solution. She didn't want to be stuck in this rut anymore, but she didn't want to let him or anyone else down. The circular thoughts almost ripped a scream from her throat.

"You still own half the company, regardless of your job title or lack thereof. If it's not going the way you want, resign." Brad slid a pen and a piece of paper across the desk. "Put it in writing, make it official, and give yourself the room to move on."

She grabbed the offerings and poised her hand to write, a formal note already building in her head. Something polite about how they had different goals, she was sorry to see their time together come to an end. When she dropped the pen instead, the question on Brad's face reflected the ones in her head.

What am I doing? "I have a different idea. Hear me out?"

"Always."

It was true. She liked to blame Brad when she

let the world bowl her over, but he *was* always there for her. "Let me consult. I'll come in with new ideas on designs, but I can't work here. Not managing, and not being driven by someone else's inspiration. You've got talented artists who can do that. I'm not your only designer anymore."

"It's going to hurt to see you go"—

His words almost broke her resolve. "I—"

—"but I think it's best for both of us. Well, maybe not as much for me, but I'm still going to use the hell out of your talent. I like my paycheck." He winked.

She gave a light laugh. "Do you still want my resignation?"

"Still? Never. I'll talk to HR and switch your paperwork over. I need you to help with the transition, though. Teach someone else the managerial side of things. Don't do it for them."

"All right." A nervous tension gurgled in her belly. She was walking away from a sure thing. About to toss aside a job many designers would kill for, so she could be whimsical and artsy. She wasn't worried about money, but she did wonder if it would be everything she hoped for. "Thank you for making time for me today."

Brad stood, stepped around the desk, and wrapped her in a tight hug. "You'd do the same for me. And I never doubt it."

They made small talk a little longer—about the wedding, about life, random things—and then she had to let him get to his next meeting. She promised to write up a job description.

As she headed outside, her heart hammered so

hard in her ribcage, she thought it might break free. But she'd done it—figured out a way at a second chance most people never got. She'd already lived her dream once. Maybe she could do it right this time.

Her confidence sapped away as she stepped outside. By the time she collapsed in her car, her hands and legs shook. Oh, God. She was going to throw up. She leaned back against the headrest, taking deep breaths until the wave of sickness passed.

She pointed the hatchback toward home and navigated almost in autopilot. Twenty minutes later, she pushed through her front door, typing out a text as she kicked off her heels.

Can I come over? She sent the message to Archer.

She hadn't finished stripping off the rest of her work clothes, when her phone buzzed with a response. *Always. Early lunch?*

Amusement whispered through her, making an odd mix with the lingering adrenaline. *Indefinite lunch.*

She stashed the suit in her closet, pulled on a pair of cutoffs and a T-shirt, and slid into the flip-flops by the front door.

Archer's reply tickled her pocket. *Explain?*

Maybe she would regret this tomorrow, but now that the nausea had faded, she felt incredible. *When I get there.*

Archer struggled to focus on work, but Tori's

messages had his thoughts in a knot. He finally turned to Derrek. "We're slow. I'll probably duck out."

"'S cool. Whatever."

Archer's neck tightened when he saw Tori's car out front. He braced himself for bad news. If she was coming over this early, her meeting with Brad couldn't have gone well. It wasn't even nine thirty. How was she finished already?

When she pushed through the front door, her smile caught him completely off guard. Was she still stuck in fake mode from her time in the office? She nodded at Derrek as she crossed the room.

What the hell? Archer's curiosity and confusion was derailed and slammed into the back of his mind when she wrapped her arms around his neck, pulled his head down, and kissed him deeply.

Derrek's whistle echoed through the room.

She broke away but didn't let go. Instead, she pulled him closer, her whisper brushing his ear. "Can we go upstairs and talk?"

His rigid cock didn't want to go anywhere and talk. It wanted to push her onto the counter, strip her those shorts off her, and make her moan. He didn't trust himself to say anything, so he settled for nodding.

She looked at Derrek again. "We'll be back." She grabbed Archer's hand and held it on her shoulder, as she tugged him behind her and prompted him to follow her up the stairs.

He couldn't take his eyes off the way her hips moved in her shorts, but he did manage to find his voice. "What's going on?"

"I quit."

"Do they know that?"

She made a noise he could only describe as an irritated grunt. "Yes, they know."

What was he supposed to say now? *Congratulations? I'm sorry? Are you feeling all right?*

She stepped into his apartment, and twirled to face him, leaning back against the door to close it. She draped her arms around his neck again and pulled him close. She rubbed her body against him and sent his blood pressure soaring.

She was testing the limits of his self-control.

"Are you all right?" he asked.

"I'm fine. I promise."

She shouldn't be like this. Why had she quit her job? And why was this bizarre giddiness so contagious? "Tell me what's going on?"

"I told you, I was tired of running. Of hiding. I wasn't happy with what I was doing, and neither I nor the job were going to change, to make things right, so I walked away."

It was what he'd wanted her to do for so long. The throb below his waist insisted he stop talking and use his mouth for something else, but the conversation wasn't over. "You look happy."

"I am."

He dipped his head to kiss her. He didn't want to hold back anymore.

"No."

He raised an eyebrow, but all he could manage was, "Hmm?"

"I need to know something first."

He nodded, laying tiny kisses along the tips of her fingers.

She let out a light laugh. "I need to know I'm not sharing you with Riley's memory."

He pulled away. She still thought that? He needed to change her belief in any way possible. *Maybe telling her would be a good place to start, dummy.* "Of course you're not. Nothing in my past could ever hope to compete with you. You're all there is."

"Promise me. Swear, whatever else happens between us, it's between us. No ghosts or skeletons."

"I promise. No Riley. Nobody but us." He kissed her again.

She sank into him, her palms on his chest and digging her fingers into his skin. He could get used to this. He cradled her neck and rested his thumb on her cheek, falling into the sensation of her lips working against his.

He slid his fingers down her spine, and she arched her back, pressing closer. Every inch of him reacted to the seduction, his skin burning for more, and his cock perking to life. He cupped her ass. She moaned against his mouth and shifted her weight.

The soft scent of her shampoo, combined with her gasps, made it difficult to think about anything but tasting her. He swept her hair aside and then shifted his attention to the seductive curve of her neck. He trailed his lips along her pale skin, drawing a line to her collarbone with his tongue.

She gripped his arm and squeezed tight, moving against him. He wanted to see her squirm with pleasure until she was spent. Friction built between his palm and her skin when he shoved her T-shirt up.

He caught the elastic of her bra on his journey and pushed it out of the way as well. Her breast bounced free. He wrapped his lips around the supple nub, flicking his tongue back and forth, and feeling her nipple harden under the attention.

He missed the banter and some of the incredible things that usually came out of her mouth when she was turned on, but her light gasps still had him as hard as he'd ever been.

He yanked off her top and tossed it aside, so he could get to her other breast. She tangled her fingers in his hair, and she held him tight when she scraped the sensitive flesh with her teeth. He growled against her skin, sinking into her heat.

He slid his hand down her stomach and dipped under the waistband of her shorts, but not lower, tracing along her stomach and hip.

She scraped his skin with her nails when she reached for his shirt, and in turn he sucked harder on her nipple. He broke away long enough to let her pull his clothing off, and then pushed her back until she hit the door.

There were still too many clothes in the way. He yanked at her shorts, and the button and zipper gave easily. He pushed the shorts and her panties to the ground, and she kicked her clothes and sandals aside.

She fumbled with his pants, and he pressed nearer to her touch. He grunted every time she brushed his rigid shaft through the denim. Seconds later, his sneakers and the rest of his clothes joined hers in a discarded pile. A sharp jolt of need spiked through him when she wrapped her fingers around his dick.

He grabbed her butt and pulled her forward, his cock between them, rubbing against her stomach. He traced over her ass cheek and between her legs. She whimpered when he dipped between her folds and brushed her opening.

He kissed along her jaw. "You're so wet."

She nudged him away, and raw disappointment filled him. He reached for her, but she held a hand against his chest and pushed him back. He started to protest, until he realized she was directing him toward the couch. She should've said so.

He grabbed her fingers and tugged her with him. "Sitting sounds like a good idea."

He dropped onto the cushions, and the rough plush dug into his bare skin, adding to his desire to bury himself inside her. He pulled her forward, but she stopped before she reached him.

She studied him, bottom lip caught between her teeth. God, she was gorgeous, full hips curving into a seductive waist, round breasts, the taunting V between her legs, and the teasing smile dancing on her face.

She straddled his legs, but she sat far enough back to keep him from doing anything except rest his hands on her hips.

"What are you up to?" He struggled to keep the question playful.

Her smile grew, but she didn't say anything. A pained groan tore from his throat when she wrapped her hand around his shaft and stroked slowly. Most delicious torture ever.

She hovered a few inches above his legs. She glided the head of his cock up her slit, and he dug his fingers into her waist at the exquisite tease. Her gasp mixed with his, when she bumped her clit with his cock.

He expected her to let him thrust inside. Instead, she continued to stroke him, using his cock against her swollen sex. Her eyes were half closed now, and her head leaned back.

He watched in heated fascination as she worked herself over, using him. She was definitely incredible.

chapter seventeen

Tori blocked out everything except the physical sensations of the now—Archer's skin against her thighs, his thick shaft in her hand, and the spark of pleasure that rocked through her every time she stroked her clit with the head of his cock.

She rocked against him. It was good, but it wasn't enough. She positioned him at her opening and then dropped down. A cry of pleasure tore from her throat when he plunged deep inside her.

"Fuck, Tori." His hands traveled up her back.

The new sensation mingled with the others, making her head swim. She didn't trust herself to speak. That entailed accessing parts of her brain she didn't want participating. But the deep current cutting through his voice heightened her arousal.

She locked her gaze on him again, losing herself in the sharp hazel staring back. She rocked against him, feeling the pressure build inside. His grunts told her he was close to climaxing. He dropped his hands to her hips again, keeping the rhythm from increasing.

She trailed her fingers down her own stomach, more heat flooding her when he followed her movement with his gaze. She dipped between her legs and found her clit. The swollen button pulsed at her touch, and her building orgasm pushed past whatever held it back.

He picked up the pace, pounding against her hard as she came. She clenched around his shaft, drawing more short groans from him. A moment later, he thrust inside her one final time and stopped.

Tori rested her head on Archer's chest, listening to his heart and panting. Cool air rushed in around her, brushing the thin sheen of sweat on her skin.

He softened and dropped out of her, and still they sat pressed together. She wasn't sure how much time passed. It was such an exhausting day. All the energy seeped from her, as safety surrounded her.

Why couldn't she stay like this forever? Just them—no work, no exes, no anything else. She was so tired of it all. Her eyes drifted shut.

"Hey." Archer's soft voice nudged the edge of her consciousness. Her eyelids refused to budge, like they'd been dipped in glue. She pried them open and blinked a few times, trying to find some moisture, before she sat up.

He traced a thumb over her cheek, watching her, his brows knit together. "I think you fell asleep."

"I'm sorry. I didn't mean to."

"It's okay. Can you stand?"

She nodded, wobbling as he helped her to her feet. He wrapped an arm around her waist and nudged her toward the bedrooms. She didn't protest when he steered her into his, instead of the guest room.

He helped her crawl into bed and climbed in

next to her. She curled up next to him. He trailed his fingers through her hair. *Damn it.* She was getting used to this. And she didn't mind at all. It would be okay. He'd promised.

♥♥♥

Archer extracted himself from Tori's sleeping form, careful not to wake her. It had been years since he'd seen her so lighthearted and stress-free. Her hair draped across her face and over the pillow, haloing out around her. *Please let her sleep well.* She deserved it.

He wanted to stay wrapped up with her, but it was early afternoon, and he had phone calls to make. The first one was on his speed dial—number three. He probably needed to bump it up a slot. That could wait, though.

"Do I answer? Do I ignore you? Do I tell you to fuck off? What would you do if you were me?" Zane's tone was flat, as it traveled over the lines.

That could've gone worse. Archer collapsed onto the couch and dropped his elbows to his knees. "Hear me out? Give a friend a chance to apologize?"

"Dude. You hit on my fiancée every fucking chance you get. One, you'd pound my face into the dirt if you were me, and two, it's not me you have to apologize to."

They were still talking; that was promising. "I know, but logic tells me she's not going to take my call. That, and I don't want the gesture misinterpreted, so I'm going through her big, bad bodyguard."

"Apologize, make it good, and I may tell Riley.

It's still not up to me to forgive you, though."

"I'm sorry." Archer acknowledged the truth of the words as he spoke them. "For not respecting her decisions, for trying to control the conversation when she came by the other day, and for being an ass, overall."

"You know what really got to her?"

Archer racked his brain. He'd covered all his bases in his apology, hadn't he? "No?"

"You wanted to have The Pie deliver."

"They have good pizza."

"Not my point. The favor she wanted to ask didn't have to do with using your shop. She wanted you to make that stupid *onigiri* and those bean-paste-filled buns you make for anime club. Not only did you not let her finish, you wanted to order cheap, greasy pizza for her book launch."

"I'm sorry. Really? She wanted me to cook? Riley can cook." Archer leaned back against the couch, flopping his head back to lock his gaze on the ceiling.

"Cookies, pot pies, sure, she can cook. But not that stuff."

"Understood. So if I apologize and promise to make snacks, I don't suppose she still needs a venue?"

"Why?" Zane sounded suspicious.

Archer winced, glad no one could see him. He hated to admit he needed help, but it had to be done. "The shop is suffering, sales are down, and I'm hoping an afternoon of your fiancée's sparkling presence and gorgeous comics will bump sales for a day or two."

"Did you just…? Are you really…?"

Archer snarled silently at the receiver. "I'm sorry I was an ass to Riley. She doesn't deserve that. I don't know what got into me, and I didn't mean anything by it. I know the two of you are happy together. A fucking blind man could see that. And I'm asking for help. Please?"

"Yeah, I'll talk to her. No guarantees, but it'll probably be fine. Especially since she already said she'd do it if you stopped being an ass."

Archer couldn't hide his growl this time. "You were already going to say *no big deal*?"

"She's a lot more forgiving than I am. And you know you deserve to grovel."

"Yeah, all right. Let me know for sure. Thanks."

"No worries." The teasing and tension evaporated and were replaced with sincerity. "Talk to you soon." Archer dropped his arms to his sides and let the phone tumble from his hand. That had gone a lot better than it could have. Now he had to convince himself he was willing to sign over his soul to Elliot. It would be better for Tori. Right? It would give her something to do, and the sponsorship offer was good money for both of them. Not that Tori needed money—that had to be a nice feeling—but she didn't want to be idle, either.

He reached for his phone but dropped his hand again at the last minute. He needed a drink or something, before he made that call.

"Come back to bed?" Tori's soft tone shattered any other thought.

He looked up to see her leaning out of the

bedroom doorway in nothing but one of his button-down shirts, with none of the buttons done up. She shifted her weight from one foot to the other, and he caught a flash of what was—and wasn't—underneath. Fuck. He was so lucky to have her. He didn't know what he would do if he lost her.

He shoved the string of thoughts to the back of his mind and smiled. "Of course."

chapter eighteen

Tori rested behind the register, grateful for the short pause between customers. The steady stream of people had kept up since Archer opened that morning. Some were there for Riley's book launch and autograph, and others stopped in to see what was going on and make sure they weren't missing out.

It was almost two now, and aside from a snatched rice ball here and there—Archer had outdone himself with the snacks—there hadn't been much time to breathe, let alone think about anything but *now*.

She wasn't getting the worst of it, though. Watching the registers was nothing, compared to what Zane and Archer had to put up with. The main characters in Riley's comic were gay, and some of the scenes were explicit.

All four of their costumes were the same— slacks, open school-uniform-style jackets, and white tank tops. Since Riley had modeled one of the main characters after Zane, fans had been asking all morning if he and Archer were a couple, and a few of the girls begged to see them kiss. Or act out one of the scenes from the book.

Both men were being good sports and coping well. Sort of. *Coping* meant they were doing their best not to be in the room at the same time, and then insisting that wasn't what they were doing when either Riley or Tori teased them about it.

Zane scooted in behind the counter and dropped another box of books on the ground. The box landed with a loud *thunk*.

He leaned back against the shelves, a few feet from her.

"You sure you don't want to hide a little longer?" She kept her tone light. "Make sure another fangirl doesn't recognize you?"

He chuckled. "I'm sure I'll be fine. Thanks for being here today."

"I wasn't doing anything else. Besides, I'm a fangirl, too." She smiled, enjoying the lighthearted atmosphere in the shop. Though she was helping Brad find her replacement, stepping away from the job left her feeling freer than she had in years. It was as if someone snapped some of the chains holding her back. She'd dive head first into taking more commissions soon, and until then, she'd enjoy her free time.

Zane shook his head, one corner of his mouth twitching up, but not quite forming a smile. "Have we ever talked like this before? I was pretty sure you didn't like me, before today."

"I didn't." Once upon a time, the accusation would have made her close off, regardless of the friendly tone. Now it felt good to have the conversation. Something told her honesty would be okay. This was a chance to clear the air.

"Past tense. I'll take that." His shoulders relaxed. Sometimes he glanced at her, but for the most part, his attention was on Riley. "Can I ask why?"

"From where I sat, you were the guy who ran away for six years, and then came back expecting everyone to act as if nothing had changed." As the words landed on her ears, she realized how much of herself she'd been projecting on him. The things she hated herself for doing, she held against someone else.

"What about now?"

Good question. Part of her was surprised to find she already knew the answer, the rest of her was grateful to finally recognize it. "I don't know your reasons, but they're your own. Besides, you and Riley are good together. Like, *really* good. Anyone can see you make each other happy."

That was the one thing she struggled with today. The shared glances between the two, the private nudges and whispers, the intimacy conveyed in a single look—they left her with a longing she couldn't ignore. *Will I ever have that?*

Archer caught her attention from across the room, a grin splitting his face when his gaze met hers.

Do I already have that?

"Besides," she continued when she realized she'd let the conversation lapse, "Riley never would have let Archer collar her."

Zane let out a tiny cough. "You noticed?"

"The white *choker* she never takes off? I noticed. But I doubt most people have."

"So we're good now?"

She nodded. "I'd still pay to see you and Archer make out." A few teasing images flashed in her head, and as something whispered under her skin, she realized she meant it.

"Pick someone else, and I'll think about it."

"I'll keep that in mind." She laughed. The crowd in the shop was swelling again, and she returned to her post at the register, while he went back to keeping Riley company at the autograph table.

Tori dove back into her work, swapping jokes and money with customers, and enjoying the afternoon.

"Quite a turn out," a familiar voice got her attention.

Tori looked up to see Gwen, a stack of books on the counter in front of her.

"It is." Tori wasn't sure what to say. She thought Gwen was kidding when she said she'd spend too much money in a place like this. The stack of books in front of her, including a couple signed by Riley, was evidence.

Gwen took a bite out of a rice ball, and chewed thoughtfully while she handed over her credit card. "Is this real plum in the middle?"

"It is. Archer's got a knack for walking the line between fun and authentic." Tori finished ringing up the purchase and slid everything into a bag.

"Really? He makes these himself?"

"He's pretty good at it."

"He's fantastic." Gwen finished the snack, wiped off her fingers, and tossed the used napkin into a nearby trash bin. "The two of you put together could get up to some incredible things."

Heat flooded Tori's cheeks at the whisper of images that came to mind. Wow. Her imagination was getting carried away this afternoon, and that wasn't what Gwen meant. Actually, she wasn't sure what Gwen meant. "How so?"

"Four words—milk-and-tea shop."

Tori had heard of the places. They were popular in Japan, but she had no idea what they had to do with her and Archer.

Gwen's purse chimed, and she grabbed her phone. "Sorry," she said to Tori, sliding her bag of books off the counter and already turning away. "We'll catch up later."

Tori shook her head at the odd conversation, not sure what to make of it.

Zane held up an empty tray. "Do we have any more of the buns?"

"Watch the register. I'll be back," Tori said.

She sprinted up the stairs to Archer's apartment, the action feeling as comfortable as anything. She'd spent as much time at his place over the last few days as she had at her own, especially making the final prep for the book party.

It only took her a few seconds to find another plastic tub filled with treats. Last one. She was glad the day turned out to be such a success.

She stepped out of the apartment and locked the door behind her, in case anyone wandered. Better safe than sorry.

"Thanks for today." Riley's voice drifted up the stairwell.

"I think I'm the one who owes you a *thank you*."

That was Archer.

Tori didn't know why, but she froze on the second step from the top. Part of her wanted to peer over the railing, and part knew it was wrong to eavesdrop. Archer had made her a promise, and she trusted him.

Riley's laugh was nervous. "I guess that makes us even."

"I guess." A long pause filled the room. Tori was about to move, when Archer spoke again. "Can I ask you something?"

"I… Sure." Riley's hesitation didn't match her words.

"Why didn't we work out?"

Archer's question rang in Tori's ears, and her stomach dropped into her feet. He hadn't. No. She sank onto the landing, legs suddenly weak. He didn't mean it that way, right?

"Does it matter?" Riley asked.

"It does to me."

Tori had to bite the inside of her cheek, to keep a whimper from slipping out. *Please, don't let him be doing this.* She was hallucinating or something.

Riley sighed. "Why? We weren't meant to be. We don't work together. Isn't that enough?"

"But we were good together. We get along, we like each other, and we have the same interests."

Tori tilted her head back, and she stared at the ceiling, blinking back the tears.

"What about Tori?" Riley asked.

"That's why I need to know."

Oh, God. Please. A sob clawed at Tori's throat, begging for release.

"What do you want me to say, Archer?" The irritation was gone from Riley's voice, replaced with something sad and quiet. "We make each other miserable. We're decent friends and lousy lovers. We never deserved a second chance, let alone a tenth or twentieth."

"Fuck." Tori couldn't listen anymore. She'd been eviscerated. She stormed down the stairs, the house shaking with each of her footsteps. When she reached the main floor, Archer and Riley both stared at her, guilt on his face and sympathy on hers.

"Let me help you out." She shoved the box of buns into his hands. "How about, *I'm not interested, Riley; I've moved on.* Or, *We both know you're happy now, and so am I?*" She couldn't keep the waver from her voice, and tears threatened to overwhelm her. "Either of those might be a good next line, Archer."

"Tori…" He took a step toward her.

Riley frowned. "I'm sorry."

"Don't." Tori didn't know who she was talking to. She couldn't blame Riley, not completely, but it didn't stop her from doing so, at least a little. She brushed past them both and made a straight line for the exit. The bell swung violently on the handle, when she pushed outside, and the howling wind tore the door from her hands. She kept going, not daring to look back.

Archer wrapped a hand around her arm. "Wait. Please?"

"Don't touch me." She jerked away and whirled to face him, fury pouring through her and steamrolling the hurt. "You promised me. Swore there was only us." She didn't give him a chance to reply. Didn't trust him or herself with whatever might come out of his mouth. "I don't know if Elliot is right about you, and you can't get over the fact Riley was the one who left, or if you're so fucked up in the head that this is fun for you.

"It doesn't matter," she said before he could interrupt. "I don't care why you did it. I trusted you with my secrets. You knew my reasons. And you stood there and lied to me about how you feel."

"Tori, please."

"No." The single word fell hard, followed by a crack of thunder and a bolt of lightning that lit up the sky. "Don't. I don't want to hear it."

chapter nineteen

Archer chased Tori as she peeled away, but slowed to a halt when she kept going. *Stupid. Stupid. Stupid.* What the hell was wrong with him? He couldn't answer his own question. Another clap of thunder tore through the sky. He didn't know why he'd said any of it. He needed to learn to keep a lid on it around Riley. If only he could remember that before he fucked up, instead of after. No wonder Tori was pissed off.

The sky opened up, and buckets of water washed over him. She had every right. What had he done? He turned to head back inside and pulled the door shut behind him before the monsoon-like weather could soak more than the entryway carpet.

Riley was back at her signing table. She looked anywhere but at him, brow furrowed as she traced lines with her thumb over her fingernails. Zane stood behind her, hands jammed in his pockets, eyes narrowed, and gaze locked on Archer, following his every step.

Archer stepped around the pair to grab a towel from the back room. He didn't know which was worse. No. Wait. He did know. It was the look on

Tori's face. The hurt in her voice. The fact that he caused it.

He rubbed his hair dry, patted the excess water from his outfit, and draped the towel around his shoulder. He couldn't look at either of his friends, as he took a spot behind the register. Not that he could actually call Zane and Riley friends anymore. When he thought about it, the three of them had tossed that label aside a long time ago. That hurt to admit. Seriously, what was wrong with him?

The storm raged outside, but the festivities drew people in for the rest of the afternoon. Closing time slid up quickly, with the steady ebb of customers acting as a buffer for the tension in the room. If anyone noticed, they didn't say anything. People laughed and joked with Riley and Zane, as she signed books, and people handed Archer cash for figurines, complimenting the refreshments, and the invisible wall stayed intact.

Archer didn't push the stragglers out after closing time, but he locked the door the moment the last one was gone.

"We need to go." Riley's comment clattered around the suddenly still room.

Archer faced her. A lot of people would be offended by what he was about to say, but neither of the people in the room with him was on that list. "I didn't mean it, you know. I'm not interested in another chance."

Riley stood and tugged her wristlet purse into place. "I don't even guess with you anymore. So no. I don't know." Without looking, she stepped back, putting herself closer to Zane, and then pulled his arms around her shoulders. "What I do know is I'm not offering. Not now, not ever. I've figured out who and what I want."

The gesture sent a roaring rush of jealousy through Archer, similar to what he'd experienced watching the two together earlier. But it wasn't because he wanted to be in Zane's place. It was because he wanted that kind of casual intimacy with Tori. Fuck. What had he done?

"One of these days, it has to stop. You have to figure things out." As he spoke, Zane traced a finger along the edge of the white suede choker Riley always wore.

Archer leaned back against the counter, swallowing his first instinct to tell his friend off.

"That's what I need. The two of you ganging up on me."

Riley bit her bottom lip, but it didn't stop her laugh from escaping. She ducked her head and leaned more into Zane.

"And don't pull me into your kinky fantasies." Great. He was doing his best to hold his shit together, and she picked the innuendo out of his statements. He glared at her.

"Really, that's never been an issue," Zane said.

Riley looked like she was struggling to hide her smile. "Besides, we can't all get off on dirty talk and exhibitionism."

"Maybe not, but you can." Archer had seen a couple of the e-mails Riley and Zane had exchanged while Zane was deployed. Oddly enough, it wasn't something that had been a part of his physical relationship with Riley. Maybe that should have clued him in a long time ago, to their incompatibility. If only it were so easy as to lay the blame on lack of clarity. Hindsight was a ruthless bastard.

Riley's smirk broke loose, and she shrugged. "Sometimes."

"I'm still not sharing." A serious edge ran through Zane's voice.

Archer rubbed his face. There was a giant gaping hole in his chest over what he'd done to Tori, but the conversation was familiar. Comfortable. He'd forgotten what it was like to joke with these two, without the looming pressure of his relationship with Riley. Then again, it was possible he was responsible for that tension.

He had to call Tori. He needed to apologize. And he prayed to anyone who might be listening that she'd hear him out, even if he didn't deserve it.

Riley squeezed Zane's hand, and then broke away. She crossed the room and stopped a few inches from Archer. She raked her blue-eyed gaze over his face, and furrowed her brow. "Do you really need me to answer your question from earlier?"

He didn't have to ask her to clarify. She meant his *why didn't we work out?* He expected his pulse to race or something, based on her proximity and the sympathy in her voice. But the excitement wasn't there. "No. I already know the answer, and even if I didn't, it doesn't matter."

She pressed her lips to his cheek, letting the kiss linger for a moment before stepping away. "Too bad we didn't figure it out sooner."

Like he needed her to tell him that. Ice from the spot she'd touched traveled through him and settled in his gut. "Yeah. Too bad."

Tori sat on her balcony, staring out beyond the mountains. Maybe if she focused hard enough, she could see home. Or where *home* had been. This was supposed to be her home now, and she didn't want to give it up.

When she ran away back then, it was because she couldn't stand up for herself. But what did speaking up do for her? Almost broke her relationship with her brother, and got her a string of lies from a man she thought liked her. The man she thought she loved. The word bounced around in her ribcage, tearing pieces of her loose with every rattle.

The rain stopped almost an hour ago, but clouds still blanketed the sky. The steady drip from the gutters on her overhang blurred the orange flame the setting sun cast on the skyline. She ran the back of her hand across her cheeks. Right. It was water causing the blur. She sniffled. This hurt so much. She didn't remember the betrayal hurting so much last time. Was it because she made the mistake twice, despite her caution?

Maybe. She didn't know. She was tired of thinking about it, and her eyes were irritated, and her throat was raw, and she still couldn't focus on anything else. Her phone buzzed again. She clenched her fist. She wouldn't pick it up and throw it into the street below.

She didn't bother to see who it was. It had been Archer every five minutes or so, for the last hour. The notes said various things. *Talk to me*, and, *Please let me know you're seeing these*, and, *Are you all right*?

The last one dug the deepest. What the hell kind of question was that? Did he expect her to be all right? And not a single note was an apology or an acknowledgment he screwed up. Not that it mattered. She didn't want to hear anything he had to say. If she hadn't overheard, who knew how much further he would have taken things?

Her phone buzzed again. They were down to less than two-minute increments now. She grabbed at the threads of irritation inside and used them to smother everything else, as she dialed his number.

He answered before the phone finished ringing once. "Tori, I—"

"Don't." She sounded hoarser than she expected. That was okay, she could go with hoarse. "What don't you understand about *I don't want to talk to you*?"

"But I—"

"This isn't an invitation for dialogue." Each word scratched her throat, and her hurt rushed back. "Don't call me. Don't text me. I'm not interested in anything you have to say."

"Please—"

"Goodbye." Her voice cracked on the last syllable. Hopefully she'd disconnected before he'd heard.

She could move. Sell her condo, take the equity, and drive as far as a hundred bucks in gas would get her. Not quite as far as it had four years ago, but it would be something. Except the thought of giving up, letting him chase her out of this place she loved, made her tense. She wouldn't do that. But she did still have one outlet. She took a long drink from the glass of water next to her and grabbed Elliot's card from her wallet. He answered quickly, tone cautious but friendly.

"Hey. This is Tori." A sudden lump in the back of her throat kept her from identifying herself as *Archer's friend.*

"Hey." His tone shifted in an instant, enthusiasm flowing in. "I'm so glad you called. Does this mean Archer talked to you?"

She cringed. It took some effort to keep her voice cheerful. "Since I don't know what you're talking about, I'm going to guess no." One more thing he'd kept from her. Not that it mattered at this point.

"Ah." A level of cheer faded in that single syllable. "Then, what can I do for you?"

It wasn't a good sign, but she needed this. She'd never forgive herself if she didn't explore this avenue. "I was wondering about that thing we talked about a while back. The sponsorship for my costumes. I'm wondering if there's anyone else you can hook me up with."

He chuckled, and a sliver of ice ran down her spine. Why was the sound so unpleasant? "You'd leave Archer high and dry like that?"

"I'm sure he'll be fine on his own." She wasn't out for blood or anything, but she wasn't going to go out of her way to help him.

"See, that's the thing he didn't tell you." Elliot dragged out the words, like he wanted to sound sorry, but nothing in his tone was. "It's an all-or-nothing deal for him. I can hook you up with someone else, but he doesn't get the contract unless you sign on. You're the money in this deal."

She wanted to focus on the compliment, but the rest of the statement left a sick hole growing in her gut. "I am?"

"You're the talent, beautiful." His voice oozed over the phone. "I've got a guy in Denver who would love to work with you. Especially if you're willing to visit occasionally and show off your goods, if you know what I mean."

She retched silently. "Elliot, is that really you?"

"Yeah, it is, love. The kid gloves are for clients, but you don't need that."

She rubbed her eyes, unsure what to say.

"So I can e-mail you the contract?" Elliot asked.

"No." She didn't have to think about it or consider the consequences. "No, you can't. Forget I called. Erase my number."

She hung up, processing the call. At least the shock muffled her grief, not that it would hold out for long. Fuck. What was wrong with the world? She was slowly losing every friend she thought she had.

A few drips hit the awning above her, and then more, and then the skies opened and poured down rain.

Tori wasn't sure how long she sat on the balcony, watching the storm hammer against the world. Too bad it wasn't washing anything inside away. God, this hurt.

The sound of her doorbell interrupted her musings, and the pounding that followed made her heart leap into her throat in surprise. What the hell?

At least she hadn't been crying. Not for a few

hours, anyway. She hoped her eyes weren't too red. She climbed from her chair and dragged her feet along the carpet, to the front door. Through the blinds, she could see a silhouette facing the front landing.

It wasn't him. It was just someone shaped like him. A neighbor. A lost pizza boy. *Oh, pizza.* She should eat. Except her stomach wasn't going to let her do that any time soon. She didn't want to fill that void.

She opened the door, and her insides twisted in on themselves when she saw Archer on the other side. Fury. Regret. Longing. She didn't even know which feeling to focus on, except she was determined to ignore any emotion that wanted to let him in.

"Go away."

He stepped forward, resting his foot on the line between inside and out. "Tori, let—"

"No." It took all of her willpower to force the word out. Too much of her wanted to listen to him. But that was what had caused the problem in the first place. "Go away."

"Not until you hear me out."

She glared at his foot. Looking directly at him hurt too much.

He inched his toes from her condo and back onto the landing. "I'll stay out here until you're ready to listen."

"You do that. I have other plans." She looked at him, eyes narrowed. She was past caring about the part of the sentiment that sounded sweet. He'd lied to her, and he'd betrayed her, and she wasn't going to spend her time on him.

She closed the door and flipped the deadbolt into place. *Turn and walk away. Head back to the couch. Turn on the TV. Pretend he isn't there.* That was all she had to do. Simple things she did every day. In five or ten minutes, he'd realize she was serious and go home.

She flopped onto the couch and flipped on the TV. She had no idea what she watched. The shadow on the other side of her blinds taunted her. Something with explosions. She needed something with explosions.

The rain drove against the side of the building and then the wind switched direction, howling through the cracks in her front window, slamming large drops of water into the glass.

She wouldn't look up. Gaze on the screen. He would go home soon. And it served him right that he was getting soaked. Five minutes passed. Then ten. And then an hour. She watched the clock tick off the seconds in time to the beat of the hammering rain.

Fuck it. She grabbed a towel from the bathroom and yanked open the front door. She shoved the towel into his arms and pulled him inside by his soaked shirt.

She shut the door behind him and leaned against it. "I'll let you talk, and then you'll go home."

He nodded. A heavy silence settled between them while he toweled off his hair and patted his clothes dry. Sort of. He still left a puddle under his feet. She didn't even care. The carpet would dry.

"I'm sorry."

It startled her, but at least he got that bit right. "So?"

"I know I haven't told you this yet, but you have to know. I don't love Riley, I don't miss her, and I don't want another chance with her. I love you."

The confession cut deep, and she couldn't tuck aside the resulting gash. The open wound filled with the negativity that had built throughout the evening. She clenched her jaw, to keep anything from coming out.

"The only reason I care she left is because I don't know what I did wrong. Not because I want her back, but because I don't want to make the same mistakes with you. I want you. I need you. I can't lose you."

Each new word tugged at her insides. A sob rose in her throat, but she swallowed it. She took a few deep breaths, to make sure she could speak without her voice cracking. "I'm not her. If you mean that, you need to be figuring out how to make us work, not what went wrong in the past."

"I know." He took a step forward, and stopped when she moved back. "I was wrong. About so much. And I lived in the past for too long, and I have you right here in front of me, and I let what happened before blind me to what we have. You're this amazing, incredible, brilliant, gorgeous woman. And I love you, and I'm so sorry."

Damn it, he needed to stop saying that… that …*L*-word. Her tentative grip on composure was sliding away. She dug her will into it and clung to its last threads. Instinct wanted to shut him out. To hide away what she was thinking.

But she couldn't stop herself from speaking her mind. "I can't trust you. Especially not around Riley.

And if I can't trust you, we don't have anything. Not even friendship." Agony wrenched her chest.

"I understand."

She yanked back the part of her that wanted to tell him it was okay. That they'd make it work. It wasn't true, though, and it wouldn't stop the pain. She tugged the door open. "I heard you out. Go home."

"Tell me how to make it better." He looked up, and locked his gaze on hers.

"I don't know if you can. I think we're beyond making things better."

"I see."

"Good night." She felt like she was sawing herself in half when she closed the door behind him. She waited a few minutes, watching his shadow through the front curtains. Her gut plummeted to the floor when he finally turned away.

She did the same, heading into the bedroom. She dropped onto the mattress, pulled her knees to her chest, and sobbed, letting each body-wrenching ache tear through her. Maybe they would rip her apart. Then she wouldn't have to deal with the mess that was her relationship with Archer.

chapter twenty

The only way Archer could take his mind off Tori was by poring over his tattered financial records. Even that only distracted him for a few minutes at a time. His chest throbbed when he stumbled across Elliot's contract. Fuck. Even if he wanted to—which was a serious possibility—he couldn't without Tori.

A new wave of guilt rushed through him the moment the thought crossed his mind. It was true he wanted to see her do something with her talent, but he couldn't suck her into a shitty contract. She deserved better than Elliot's offer.

The door chimed, drawing his attention away from the discouraging numbers. It was Gwen. Was she there to bitch at him on Tori's behalf? That couldn't be the case, but a bit of him hoped. It would mean Tori hadn't forgotten about him.

He pasted on a smile and gave her his full attention. Easy enough, since she was the only person in the shop. "Can I help you?"

"I hope so. I really hope you still have that VF-1J… and you do."

The transforming plane from a decades-old

cartoon? He hadn't expected that. "Yeah. It's the kind of thing people always want to see, but never want to buy." Once they saw the four-hundred dollar price tag, most of them were reluctant to even touch the box for fear they might break it.

"I do."

"Excuse me?" He blinked and shook his head. There was no way he'd heard her right.

"I want the model. It's fully transformable, right?"

He pulled the box off the top shelf. Had he fallen asleep doing accounting? This was too surreal. "All three modes."

She paid without batting an eye when he told her the total, her gaze wandering around the store while he found a bag big enough for the box. She turned back to him, studying him for a moment before speaking. "How long do you have?"

"For...?" This definitely wasn't real, because he had no idea what she meant.

"Until you lose this place."

"Is it that obvious?"

She rested the bag on the floor. "Probably not to most people, but you tend to wear a look of permanent gloom. And your shelves are a little barren."

"It's been better, but it's been worse, too." The gloomy look was only partly related to the shop, but he didn't want to share with this almost stranger. Hell, he didn't know if he wanted to share much of anything with her. Like that her purchase would pay his power bill next month.

"As long as you're going to be around for a

while. We need more places like yours."

Something about the way she phrased the statement snapped his leash on propriety—or maybe it was because he was dealing with so much. "Actually, business sucks. I've got a year at the outside, and that's only if I cut my own salary and manage to keep renters in the two apartments on the middle floor." Not a lot of reliable renters wanted to live above a comic book store. "There's an option on the table, but I have to make some concessions that aren't mine to make, in order to take it. And that's only if I even wanted to."

"Can I ask what kind of option?"

"You can see for yourself if you want." It wasn't appropriate for him to talk money with anyone but his accountant, but he didn't care anymore. He plucked Elliot's contract from the stack of paperwork and slid it across the counter.

She grabbed the contract and skimmed it. Occasionally she raised her brows, or made a clucking noise with her tongue. A few minutes later, she handed it back. "You're thinking about signing this?"

"It doesn't matter whether or not I want to. The offer isn't valid without—" He snapped his mouth shut before he could spill more. He really didn't want to get into anything about Tori. His business was his to talk about, but he didn't have any right to spill her life.

"I read the last few pages. If that wasn't a condition, would you sign so much away?"

He knew what she was talking about. Even though the contract said all he had to do now was give the comic company top billing in his shop, that he didn't have to get rid of anyone else's books or toys, there was a loophole that could eventually turn the shop into whatever Elliot's company wanted. "I need the money. They're offering a steady revenue stream. The possibility of them forcing me out eventually is better than being forced out now."

"Is it really?"

His gut sank. No, it wasn't. But he didn't have another choice.

"That's what I thought," she said. "Can I ask you something?"

"Sure." Since he'd pretty much told her everything already, he wasn't sure what it would hurt.

"Why haven't you ever expanded?"

He stared at her for a moment, looking for a hint she was joking. Had she missed the rest of the conversation? "If I can't afford one store—and I own the property here—how am I supposed to open a second one?"

"You misunderstand. You're a talented chef; those bean-paste buns the other day were incredible. Have you seen those milk-and-tea shops popping up around the country?"

"I've heard a little." Some of the people in anime club had talked about one in Detroit, after getting back from a convention there. The place had been modeled after a similar trend in Japan. The waiters and waitresses all wore costumes, and the entire thing was supposed to be a combination of good food, a fun atmosphere, and a feeling of being in Japan without having to leave the US.

"The house is already wired for electricity and has water. You've got kitchens in each apartment, and you have access to a brilliant costume designer. What's stopping you from adding something like that to your store?"

The idea hadn't occurred to him. That was the first thing stopping him. But now that it was bouncing in his head… The brilliant costume designer he knew wouldn't have anything to do with him. And he wasn't even worried about the business implications.

How was he going to make things right? He tucked the thought away as best he could—which wasn't really at all—to get back to the conversation. "I don't have any space for something like a café."

She nodded at the series of tables at the far end of the room, and another ache tore through him with the memory of his first time with Tori. God, he missed her.

He swallowed back the thought. "I like to keep it in reserve, in case anyone wants to tabletop game."

"So set up a few smaller tables, some more chairs, and let them use some of them if anyone has the urge. You've got room behind the counter for an espresso machine. Install a sandwich press or microwave, or serve those rice balls and such cold."

The idea was tempting. The more she talked, the more he liked it. But that didn't mean it was practical. "Even if I wanted to do it, I can't afford those kinds of changes. Not now."

"I'll invest." She didn't hesitate.

"I… Uh… What?" He couldn't have heard her right. "This isn't the kind of venture you make a lot of money from."

"I'm not in it for the money, though I certainly won't complain about the return." She nodded toward the bag at her feet. "I told you, we need more places like this. I get tired of diner food. This gives me a new place to stop for a cup of coffee, because now that I've been in here, I'm going to blow most of my wallet on toys until Brad stops me.

"Besides, *invest* probably wasn't the right word. Think of it more as a loan. I'll be a silent partner as long as you're making your monthly payments, and in five years, you'll be out of debt if you run things right."

"So what makes your offer better than this one?" He nodded at the contract on the counter. "No offense, but how do I know I'm any safer with you?"

"Smart man. No wonder Tori likes you. We'll put it all in writing, have a lawyer look it over, and it'll all be in the contract. You don't sign unless you're comfortable with it."

It was too good to be true, but that didn't stop him from clinging to the idea. He wanted it, and he liked it, and he only saw one other issue with it. "I don't have access to a costume designer, though." Didn't she already know that?

"I thought…" She pursed her lips. "I won't ask for details. But regardless of what happened between the two of you, I'll be your go-between. Contract her independently. I hear from a reliable source she's doing that now. You can do it without her, too. But she's got skill, and your wait staff would look good in her outfits."

Tori did have skill. He never denied that. He

also couldn't deny that, regardless of how hard he tried, he couldn't stop thinking about her. "Give me some time to think about it."

"You know where to find me when you decide. Don't take too long."

"Or the offer expires?" His body tensed.

She gave him a look he could only describe as confounded. "Or you won't have a shop left to expand. You already told me your time was short."

"Right." He leaned back against the counter. "Of course. I'll let you know soon."

Tori paced the length of her condo. She was surprised she hadn't worn a rut in the floor yet. Almost two weeks of her new *consulting* position, and she was going out of her mind with boredom. She needed to reach out to some commission contacts. She needed to dive more into the search. Her gaze fell on the dress form in the corner and the costume hanging next to it, from Riley's book launch.

She needed to get over an entire chapter of her life. What had she been thinking? Sleeping with a guy she wasn't dating, daydreaming about making what she wanted instead of what people paid for, wishing she had a life she wasn't meant for. An unwanted wave of sorrow swept over her. She wanted Archer back.

No, she didn't. She was fine. She'd get over him. She didn't miss him so much it kept her up at night and made every bit of her ache from the memories.

A knock echoed through her apartment, and her heart leaped. Would it be Archer? Stupid, *stupid* thought. Why would she want to see him? If it was him, the conversation wouldn't last long.

Disappointment flickered through her when she saw Riley.

"I know I'm not who you want to see, but I have to apologize." Riley's smile was weak.

Tori let her in and turned away. "You didn't do anything wrong."

"I did. I egged him on. I shouldn't have pushed. I'm sorry."

Damn it. Tori had managed to hold back the tears for a couple of days. She didn't need them coming back now. She blinked away the sting in her eyelids before facing Riley again. "At least I found out now. Before anything happened."

Like the confession of love he made a few hours after. Or a commitment, since she'd already given everything else to him. She choked back a sob. No, she hadn't. She was being melodramatic.

So then, why did it hurt so much?

"I guess." Riley traced a finger around her collar. "I was also wondering if you'd be willing to take a commission from me?"

Commission. The word stuck in Tori's brain. It didn't wipe away the sorrow, but it did distract her for a moment. "For…?"

"We have pictures posted on the website of the release party, and the comments and e-mails are starting to choke the servers." Riley laughed. "I need to know if you can make me more outfits. Charge me whatever you normally would, and I'd love your input on new designs. I need a couple for giveaways. And maybe more than a couple of the collars. People really love those."

She couldn't be hearing right. Actual creative work? She wanted to assure Riley it was okay, she'd make them and only charge for materials, but the business part of her brain kicked in, and for once, Tori allowed it full rein. "I'll give you a discount if you link back to me."

"Do you have something to link back to? Because I would do that in a heartbeat." Riley tugged her toward the couch, a glint sparkling in her blue eyes. "Are you going full time? What about your job?"

Tori pulled away. She'd never been a fan of how physical Riley was. Today, it was an even more painful reminder of Archer and all the things Tori must have done wrong. Of all the ways she was different from Riley.

She dropped into an easy chair across from Riley. "I've scaled back on my at-work responsibilities."

"Are you serious? That's amazing. Working for yourself, charging more, and getting paid every time someone makes an order."

Except ninety-nine percent of her customers came from the one place she was never stepping foot in again. Her sorrow returned in a single rush. She fiddled with the edge of the cushion beneath her. "Can I ask you something?"

"Of course."

"You and Zane. How did you know?"

Riley shifted in her seat, not meeting Tori's

gaze. "We've both known for a long time, but we were really good at ignoring it. One day, it hit me, and I had to tell him. Not saying something—the regret associated with it—would slowly consume my soul and sanity."

And Tori thought *she* was melodramatic. Despite the fact she wanted to be disgusted by the sappiness, she adored it. And she hated herself for not being capable of the same thing.

"I'm sorry." Riley flopped back against the couch. "That probably doesn't help you any. I overheard everything you said to Archer. I know you've already told him, and he threw it back at you."

Tori winced. She hadn't told him, though. She'd said she didn't want to share him with Riley's memory. Beyond that, she'd never told him how much she wanted him, or how he haunted her dreams. This was the first time she'd even allowed herself to dwell on the idea of love.

"You never told him." Riley's voice was flat.

"I did." Tori's defensiveness kicked in on instinct. "Sort of. I said a lot of other things. He could have assumed."

"Oh, he's good at that. But never trust him to assume the right thing."

"Like you're so perfect?"

Riley held up her hands. "Not even close. It's an opinion. But if you never told him, you really can't expect him to know. You can't expect that from anyone."

"What am I going to do?" Tori leaned her head back, to stare at the ceiling.

A few seconds later, Riley's face appeared in

front of her, looking down, compassion in her eyes. "I have a lot of opinions, and normally I'd give them to you, but it doesn't matter what I think. You have to do what you want to do."

Tori cringed, and the pain inside throbbed as much as it had the day it moved in. She knew exactly what she wanted to do, but it wasn't practical. Any of it. Especially since she didn't know if she could trust Archer again.

chapter twenty-one

Archer slumped in his desk chair. He was glad Derrek was on the clock today, watching the front counter. With any luck, he could keep it that way a bit longer. He stared at the paperwork in front of him. He had Gwen draw up a contract. His lawyer looked at it—he'd be paying that bill off for a while—and it was all legit. Except for the bit about the costumes. The details weren't in the contract. How he got them was up to him. Gwen had offered again to talk to Tori, if he no longer had that option.

But he had to give it another try. He had to call Tori. No, he had to show up on her doorstep again. Not because of the business stuff; they could talk about that later. If there was a chance. He had to… What?

A knock cut through his thoughts before they could build steam, and he looked up. His heart leaped when he saw Tori, and then plummeted at her flat expression.

She wore a denim skirt that only reached halfway down her thighs, and her T-shirt hugged every inch of her torso perfectly. And she was very distinctly keeping her distance, as much as was possible in the small room. The corners of her eyes tugged down. "Can we talk?"

Yes. Definitely yes. He gestured to a chair. "Have a seat."

She closed the door and leaned against it, instead of sitting.

"Tori, I'm so, so—"

"Me first." Her voice wavered. "Please, let me say what I need to. If you really have to interrupt, I can't stop you, but I need to get this out."

The empty pit, which had moved into his chest, wasn't sure what to do. Moan some more about being empty or slink away. He gave her a small smile. "Of course."

She clenched and unclenched her hand. "I love you." The words tumbled out in a single blur.

He couldn't have heard her right. Should he ask her to repeat herself? Was he projecting? He didn't get a chance to reply.

She stood straighter. "I love you." There was no mistaking the words that time. They echoed in the tiny box of a room. "It's not something I can simply cut off. And I know I wasn't supposed to fall, it was just supposed to be sex, and I did anyway, and it— you mean so much more to me than a couple of tumbles. When I said I didn't want any ghosts between us, I should have been more specific, and that's my fault, but I'm telling you now, and I meant it, and I mean this and… Do with it what you will. But I had to tell you."

The empty pit slid away, something bright taking its place. There was still an ache, but he was pretty sure this wasn't a bad one. He wasn't positive—it was a new sensation for him—but he was willing to give it a chance. He was on his feet in an instant, stepping toward her. "You know I love you, too."

"There's a problem though." She held up a hand and rested her palm flat on his chest, and stopped him from closing the distance. The flatness was gone from her expression, replaced with a frown. That didn't look right. "I miss you desperately, and I love you so much, and I still don't know how to fix this thing between us."

The words dug deep. He wanted to argue. Wanted to fall to his knees and insist there was no one but her. He wrapped his fingers around the delicate hand on his chest and pulled it away, not letting go and not stepping closer. A bit of relief joined his frustration when she didn't yank away from his touch.

"I love you so much, and I would do anything for you. I meant what I said the other night." He poured all of his sincerity into the words.

The hard lines in her forehead softened, and a smile crept onto her face. She moved nearer to him.

His hope poked its head again and peered around. He pressed forward. "I was wrong. About Riley, about Elliot… about so much. And I want to make it up to you, if you give me a chance."

"I guess." Her tone was reluctant, but her seductive smirk contradicted it. She draped her arms around his neck and nudged him back with her body. "If you really want to make it up to me, I know a good way to start."

He rested his hands at the small of her back,

holding her captive. Every nerve in his body came alive, raw from the sudden shift in moods, and looking for an outlet. He dipped his head and kissed her hard, crushing his lips against his teeth, and memorizing each curve and contour pressed against him. They broke apart with a gasp. "You know Derrek's not that far away, right?" he asked.

"And your point is? What happened to doing anything?"

He nipped at her shoulder. He adored how wicked she was. "I still will. Anything you tell me."

"I'm aware." She tilted her head back, giving him easier access to her neck. She sighed when he kissed up the soft skin. "I missed this."

He had, too. Everything about her, from her soft scent to the sounds that tore from her throat, made him want to strip her down, push her on the desk, and make her scream. But it was more important to draw the moment out and give her whatever she asked for.

She tugged at the bottom of his shirt, scraping his waist with her nails and sending tremors of want through him. "This is in the way."

He tugged the shirt over his head, not caring when he felt something on it give and tear, and then tossed it aside.

She looked him over, brown eyes appreciative. "Better." She trailed her fingers along his bare chest, making his pulse scream. With every light kiss she placed on his skin, his cock grew another degree harder. When she flicked her tongue out and brushed his nipple, he thought he might explode.

She stepped back, one corner of her mouth tugged up in a mischievous grin. She grabbed the bottom of her shirt and discarded it. Her hair tumbled around her shoulders in soft waves, caressing the top of a lacy bra.

Gaze never leaving his face, she reached behind her. Seconds later, the cups holding her breasts tumbled loose, and she let the white lingerie drop onto a nearby chair.

He grabbed her fingers and tugged her to him again. He rested his palm on her stomach, and then slid it lower. "I love watching you."

"Convenient. I love being watched." Her laugh was light and teasing.

He kissed her again, memorizing every inch of her lips against his. He pushed his tongue into her mouth, and it danced and intertwined with hers. She shifted her weight against him, bare breasts caressing his chest.

He glided his hand up her ribcage. Her skin was smooth under his palm. He cupped a plump mound and kneaded softly. Every whimper tearing from her throat hit a gorgeous note.

She used her body to move him, turning them both until she was behind his desk, back to his chair. She nudged him away, and disappointment washed over him when all contact between them broke. His fingers twitched by his side, begging to reach for her.

She slid her thumbs up her legs, pushed up the edges of her denim skirt, and then bent at the waist, to drag her panties down.

His cock throbbed inside his jeans, straining to feel her when she held the undergarment up. She tossed it on his desk. Never touching him, she whispered in his ear, "I want to feel your mouth on my pussy."

"Let me taste you, then." He loved hearing her talk like that, and he was ready to drop to his knees for her.

She pushed onto the edge of his desk. She hooked her finger into his belt and tugged.

He tangled his fingers in her hair and yanked her head back, to kiss her hard. Her teeth scraped his bottom lip. She rested her hands on his shoulders and pushed him away, coaxing him to kneel.

chapter twenty-two

Tori knew things weren't all better. She and Archer still needed to spend time cementing their words and rebuilding misplaced trust. But she knew they were both going to try. And the slick want between her legs made a compelling case that feeling him inside her was an important part of the process.

Archer didn't resist when she nudged him to the ground. When he trailed a finger up the inside of her thigh, it was like he'd plucked a string, and she felt the chord through her entire body.

He grazed her skin with his lips, and she whimpered. "God, Archer."

He kissed higher, pushing her legs apart as he moved. Her skirt crept up to her hips when she spread for him. He paused short of his goal, making her wetter with anticipation.

"You're so gorgeous. Every inch of you." He traced up her slit, his voice lined with gravel.

The words were sweet and full of innuendo, and they made her sex throb. She rested her weight on her palms and wrists, leaning back. "Please?"

He caressed the soft skin of her thighs with his thumbs and flicked his tongue over her vulva. She gasped at the sensation. He licked higher, but never to her swollen center.

"You're such a tease." She forced the words through clenched teeth. "Suck my clit."

He complied, wrapping his lips around her sex. He licked the sensitive nub, each bump sending another wave of pleasure through her. She tangled her fingers in his hair and ground against his face.

Her climax built but evened off before she reached the peak. She gasped and slid against his attention. She should hold out longer, but she didn't have the patience. "I'm so close," she panted. "Fuck me with your fingers."

He nudged the edge of her opening, prodded it with two fingers, and then shoved them inside. She threw her head back, biting her bottom lip to keep from crying out. She thrust against him as she came, orgasm tearing through her and pussy clenching around him.

His attention slowed, and he pulled away. She tugged him to his feet and kissed him hard, tasting herself on his lips. With his still slick fingers, he sought out her breast. Pinching the nipple. Slid off.

With his other hand, he tugged back her head. His gaze locked on hers, something dark and seductive raging underneath. He growled, "My turn."

Her lower gut clenched at the combination of the threat and promise, and she nodded. He squeezed her tit, and her sex perked to life again, still tender but wanting whatever he had in mind.

He sucked hard on her neck, teeth scraping the skin, sending chutes of pain and pleasure through her. When he finally let up, he slid his mouth to her ear. He nipped at the lobe before talking. "I'm so hard right now, it hurts."

He pressed between her legs until her mound rested against his jeans and the hard length underneath. "And I want to bury my dick inside you and then pound you until you forget anyone exists besides us. Until I have to swallow your cries as you come."

The power behind his words, and every forceful syllable, made her still-tender opening beg for more. "Fuck me."

He chuckled and put enough space between them to undo his jeans. She scooted her hips to feel more, when he brushed the head of his cock along her slit. He reached her opening and forced inside her without further warning.

She gasped at the sensation of being spread apart so abruptly, and she pushed hard against him. He rested his hands at her hips, digging his thumbs into her as his slow rhythm built into something fast and frantic.

He hooked his hands under her legs and lifted her knees, pressing them to her chest. She had to lean all of her weight on her hands to keep her balance. Every time he drove inside her, he bumped her G-spot.

"Jesus, Archer. You feel so good." She slammed her ass against his hips as another orgasm built inside.

He dropped her legs. He pressed his chest against hers, and he sought out her breast again. He rolled her nipple between his fingers, and his lips brushed her ear. "Come for me."

He pressed his lips to hers as he pounded her hard, pinching the swollen flesh of her tit. The combination of sensations filled her head and climax swept over her. She screamed into his mouth as she came, his kisses muffling the sound.

He didn't let up in his rhythm, drawing out her climax. He settled both hands on her hips again and kissed along her shoulder. His grunts echoed through her skin. He sank his teeth into her flesh, and the new sensation made her opening clench around his cock.

He pounded one more time and slowed to a stop as a shudder ran through him. He kissed the bite marks on her shoulder and neck, panting as he spoke. "I think I left a mark."

"Good. Something for me to show off." She slouched forward against him when her arms threatened to give out

He looked up and locked his gaze on hers, a smile threatening to split his face. "God, I love you."

"And don't you forget it." The words sent a new kind of warmth through her, and she returned the grin.

"Never."

Tori brushed a hand over the back of her skirt, making sure it was hanging straight. Not that the maid costume covered very much of her behind. It hinted at what might be underneath without revealing anything.

She gave the contents of Archer's fridge one last glance, before swinging the door shut. Extra gallons of milk and cartons of cream lined every spot.

In the month since they officially hooked up, life had been a whirlwind of insanity.

She didn't mind the sex part of the bedlam, or really any of it, but it did make her head spin. She made costumes, he hired waiters and waitresses, and together, they managed to spend a large chunk of Gwen's loan on things like licenses, converting one of the middle-floor apartments into a commercial-worthy kitchen, and turning one corner of his comic shop into a café.

In about half an hour, they were opening the doors on their new venture. She'd be waiting tables. Riley and Zane had volunteered to help, except they'd be in their school uniforms from Riley's comic signing. Tori thought about doing the same, but she liked the excuse to wear the frilly maid outfit.

Nervous excitement churned in her gut. She grabbed a glass from the cupboard, filled it in the sink, and downed the water in a single swallow.

As she set the glass on the counter, a pair of hands rested on her hips. Archer kissed the outside edge of her ear. "Hey, gorgeous. Here alone?"

She couldn't hide her grin at the cheesy line. She spun, pulling his hands back to her hips as soon as she was facing him. He'd opted for street clothes, and she didn't blame him. He had a lot more to cover than tables.

She ducked her head, hoping it looked playful and shy at the same time. "My boyfriend was here, but he abandoned me."

He pressed closer, positioning his foot between hers. "I can't fathom the logic there. How did he take his eyes off you long enough to leave? Especially in that outfit. Or out of it."

The light teasing pushed away her tension. It was corny, but it was fun. "Are you trying to get me out of my clothes?"

He traced a finger down the side of her cheek. "Will it make you forget about this missing guy of yours?"

"I don't know." She drew her finger along the edge of her neckline. "I don't even know what kind of kisser you are. And you've got a lot to live up to. He's a pretty good kisser."

He raised his eyebrows, and his lips twitched with a smile. "I'm better."

"Prove it."

He dipped his head and brushed his lips over hers, barely making contact. His hand rested at the back of her neck, holding her captive, and he deepened the kiss. She groaned and slid against him as every inch of her came alive.

They broke apart, but he kept her back pressed to the counter, his gaze locked on her face. "Well? Can I replace the schmuck who abandoned you?"

"Sorry. Thing is I really love him, and a kiss isn't everything."

His expression went flat. Had she pushed the teasing too far? His hands found her hips again, and she gasped when he lifted her to sit on the edge of the counter.

"How about this, then?" He reached in his pocket and pulled out a small, black box.

Her pulse leaped. A whisper in the back of her head asked if this could possibly be…

No. It couldn't. Could it?

"Tori"—his tone was quiet, but even—"you mean the world to me. I love you so very much, and I couldn't have asked for a better partner, in life or business."

Her heart hammered in her ribcage with each word and sentence.

"And I know sometimes I'm an ass, and sometimes I'm a pain to deal with." He opened the box.

Her mouth twisted in amusement at what was inside. He was going to babble if she let him. She leaned forward and kissed him hard. "Spit it out."

He gave a nervous laugh. "Will you marry me?"

"Yes." Her reply came out softer than she intended. "Yes. Absolutely yes," she said with more strength. She kissed him again.

He slipped the ring on her finger. It was green, plastic, and had a lantern shaped symbol in the middle. "I want you to be there to pick out your ring, so this is a stand-in."

She held up her hand, admiring the plastic trinket. "I love it. I can't wait to show it off."

He nudged her legs apart and slid between them. He held her close. "Now can I see you without the dress on?"

She laughed and used her body to push him back, as she hopped off the edge of the counter and stood again. She draped her arms around his neck and kissed him deeply. "We have a café to open." The green plastic seemed to glint in the kitchen light. "Besides, I have to show off and brag."

He pushed up the edge of her skirt and traced the elastic of her panties, sending a pleasant chill through her. Damn it, why did they have places to be?

He ran his mouth up the side of her cheek. "I'll behave for now. But don't plan on keeping the dress on for long, after I lock the doors tonight."

She laughed and pushed him back. "I wouldn't have it any other way."

Tori knew things weren't all better. She and Archer still needed to spend time cementing their words and rebuilding misplaced trust. But she knew they were both going to try. And the slick want between her legs made a compelling case that feeling him inside her was an important part of the process.

Archer didn't resist when she nudged him to the ground. When he trailed a finger up the inside of her thigh, it was like he'd plucked a string, and she felt the chord through her entire body.

He grazed her skin with his lips, and she whimpered. "God, Archer."

He kissed higher, pushing her legs apart as he moved. Her skirt crept up to her hips when she spread for him. He paused short of his goal, making her wetter with anticipation.

"You're so gorgeous. Every inch of you." He traced up her slit, his voice lined with gravel.

The words were sweet and full of innuendo, and they made her sex throb. She rested her weight on her palms and wrists, leaning back. "Please?"

He caressed the soft skin of her thighs with his thumbs and flicked his tongue over her vulva. She gasped at the sensation. He licked higher, but never to her swollen center.

"You're such a tease." She forced the words through clenched teeth. "Suck my clit."

He complied, wrapping his lips around her sex. He licked the sensitive nub, each bump sending another wave of pleasure through her. She tangled her fingers in his hair and ground against his face.

Her climax built but evened off before she reached the peak. She gasped and slid against his attention. She should hold out longer, but she didn't have the patience. "I'm so close," she panted. "Fuck me with your fingers."

He nudged the edge of her opening, prodded it with two fingers, and then shoved them inside. She threw her head back, biting her bottom lip to keep from crying out. She thrust against him as she came, orgasm tearing through her and pussy clenching around him.

His attention slowed, and he pulled away. She tugged him to his feet and kissed him hard, tasting herself on his lips. With his still slick fingers, he sought out her breast. Pinching the nipple. Slid off.

With his other hand, he tugged back her head. His gaze locked on hers, something dark and seductive raging underneath. He growled, "My turn."

Her lower gut clenched at the combination of the threat and promise, and she nodded. He squeezed her tit, and her sex perked to life again, still tender but wanting whatever he had in mind.

He sucked hard on her neck, teeth scraping the skin, sending chutes of pain and pleasure through her. When he finally let up, he slid his mouth to her ear. He nipped at the lobe before talking. "I'm so hard right now, it hurts."

He pressed between her legs until her mound rested against his jeans and the hard length underneath. "And I want to bury my dick inside you and then pound you until you forget anyone exists besides us. Until I have to swallow your cries as you come."

The power behind his words, and every forceful syllable, made her still-tender opening beg for more.

"Fuck me."

He chuckled and put enough space between them to undo his jeans. She scooted her hips to feel more, when he brushed the head of his cock along her slit. He reached her opening and forced inside her without further warning.

She gasped at the sensation of being spread apart so abruptly, and she pushed hard against him. He rested his hands at her hips, digging his thumbs into her as his slow rhythm built into something fast and frantic.

He hooked his hands under her legs and lifted her knees, pressing them to her chest. She had to lean all of her weight on her hands to keep her balance. Every time he drove inside her, he bumped her G-spot.

"Jesus, Archer. You feel so good." She slammed her ass against his hips as another orgasm built inside.

He dropped her legs. He pressed his chest against hers, and he sought out her breast again. He rolled her nipple between his fingers, and his lips brushed her ear. "Come for me."

He pressed his lips to hers as he pounded her hard, pinching the swollen flesh of her tit. The combination of sensations filled her head and climax swept over her. She screamed into his mouth as she came, his kisses muffling the sound.

He didn't let up in his rhythm, drawing out her climax. He settled both hands on her hips again and kissed along her shoulder. His grunts echoed through her skin. He sank his teeth into her flesh, and the new sensation made her opening clench around his cock.

He pounded one more time and slowed to a stop

as a shudder ran through him. He kissed the bite marks on her shoulder and neck, panting as he spoke. "I think I left a mark."

"Good. Something for me to show off." She slouched forward against him when her arms threatened to give out

He looked up and locked his gaze on hers, a smile threatening to split his face. "God, I love you."

"And don't you forget it." The words sent a new kind of warmth through her, and she returned the grin.

"Never."

♥♥♥

Tori brushed a hand over the back of her skirt, making sure it was hanging straight. Not that the maid costume covered very much of her behind. It hinted at what might be underneath without revealing anything.

She gave the contents of Archer's fridge one last glance, before swinging the door shut. Extra gallons of milk and cartons of cream lined every spot. In the month since they officially hooked up, life had been a whirlwind of insanity.

She didn't mind the sex part of the bedlam, or really any of it, but it did make her head spin. She made costumes, he hired waiters and waitresses, and together, they managed to spend a large chunk of Gwen's loan on things like licenses, converting one of the middle-floor apartments into a commercial-worthy kitchen, and turning one corner of his comic shop into a café.

In about half an hour, they were opening the

doors on their new venture. She'd be waiting tables. Riley and Zane had volunteered to help, except they'd be in their school uniforms from Riley's comic signing. Tori thought about doing the same, but she liked the excuse to wear the frilly maid outfit.

Nervous excitement churned in her gut. She grabbed a glass from the cupboard, filled it in the sink, and downed the water in a single swallow.

As she set the glass on the counter, a pair of hands rested on her hips. Archer kissed the outside edge of her ear. "Hey, gorgeous. Here alone?"

She couldn't hide her grin at the cheesy line. She spun, pulling his hands back to her hips as soon as she was facing him. He'd opted for street clothes, and she didn't blame him. He had a lot more to cover than tables.

She ducked her head, hoping it looked playful and shy at the same time. "My boyfriend was here, but he abandoned me."

He pressed closer, positioning his foot between hers. "I can't fathom the logic there. How did he take his eyes off you long enough to leave? Especially in that outfit. Or out of it."

The light teasing pushed away her tension. It was corny, but it was fun. "Are you trying to get me out of my clothes?"

He traced a finger down the side of her cheek. "Will it make you forget about this missing guy of yours?"

"I don't know." She drew her finger along the edge of her neckline. "I don't even know what kind of kisser you are. And you've got a lot to live up to. He's a pretty good kisser."

He raised his eyebrows, and his lips twitched with a smile. "I'm better."

"Prove it."

He dipped his head and brushed his lips over hers, barely making contact. His hand rested at the back of her neck, holding her captive, and he deepened the kiss. She groaned and slid against him as every inch of her came alive.

They broke apart, but he kept her back pressed to the counter, his gaze locked on her face. "Well? Can I replace the schmuck who abandoned you?"

"Sorry. Thing is I really love him, and a kiss isn't everything."

His expression went flat. Had she pushed the teasing too far? His hands found her hips again, and she gasped when he lifted her to sit on the edge of the counter.

"How about this, then?" He reached in his pocket and pulled out a small, black box.

Her pulse leaped. A whisper in the back of her head asked if this could possibly be…

No. It couldn't. Could it?

"Tori"—his tone was quiet, but even—"you mean the world to me. I love you so very much, and I couldn't have asked for a better partner, in life or business."

Her heart hammered in her ribcage with each word and sentence.

"And I know sometimes I'm an ass, and sometimes I'm a pain to deal with." He opened the box.

Her mouth twisted in amusement at what was inside. He was going to babble if she let him. She leaned forward and kissed him hard. "Spit it out."

He gave a nervous laugh. "Will you marry me?"

"Yes." Her reply came out softer than she intended. "Yes. Absolutely yes," she said with more strength. She kissed him again.

He slipped the ring on her finger. It was green, plastic, and had a lantern shaped symbol in the middle. "I want you to be there to pick out your ring, so this is a stand-in."

She held up her hand, admiring the plastic trinket. "I love it. I can't wait to show it off."

He nudged her legs apart and slid between them. He held her close. "Now can I see you without the dress on?"

She laughed and used her body to push him back, as she hopped off the edge of the counter and stood again. She draped her arms around his neck and kissed him deeply. "We have a café to open." The green plastic seemed to glint in the kitchen light. "Besides, I have to show off and brag."

He pushed up the edge of her skirt and traced the elastic of her panties, sending a pleasant chill through her. Damn it, why did they have places to be?

He ran his mouth up the side of her cheek. "I'll behave for now. But don't plan on keeping the dress on for long, after I lock the doors tonight."

She laughed and pushed him back. "I wouldn't have it any other way."

The End

www.ingramcontent.com/pod-product-compliance
Lightning Source LLC
Chambersburg PA
CBHW050527190726
48284CB00003B/973